PROCEED
WITH
CAUTION

STORIES AND A NOVELLA

PATRICIA RATTO

TRANSLATED BY
ANDREA G. LABINGER

SCHAFFNER PRESS
TUCSON, ARIZONA

The stories in this collection originally appeared in different form in the following publications:

"Rara Avis," "Chinese Boy," "As If The World Were Ending," "Neko Café," and "The Guest" originally published in Spanish as "Rara Avis," "Muchacho Chino," "Como si se acabara el mundo," "Neko café," and "El invitado" in the collection Faunas © 2017 by Adriana Hidalgo Editora, Francisco de Vittoria 2324, Planta Baja, Ciudad De Buenos Aires, Argentina

Submerged originally published in Spanish as *Trasfondo* © 2012 by Adriana Hidalgo Editora, Francisco de Vittoria 2324, Planta Baja, Ciudad De Buenos Aires, Argentina

"Black Dog" originally published in Spanish as "Perro negro" in the anthology GOL-PES, *MEMORIAS DE LA DICTADURA* © 2016 by Planeta-Seix Barral, Av. Diagonal, 662-664, 08034 Barcelona

"Quintay" was originally published in Spanish in Hispamerica: Journal of Literature at the University of Maryland (Year XLVII, No. 140, 201) and in Summer Supplement 12 of the Argentine newspaper Página 12 (January, 2019)

"Proceed With Caution" was originally published in Spanish in Summer Supplement 12 of the Argentine newspaper Página 12 (January, 2020)

First English Language Edition
Trade Paperback Original
Cover and Interior Design by Evan Johnston

Contact: Permissions Dept., Schaffner Press, POB 41567
Tucson, AZ 85717

ISBN: 978-1-943156-84-9 (Paperback)

ISBN: 978-1-943156-85-6 (PDF)
ISBN: 978-1-943156-85-6 (EPub)

ISBN: 978-1-943156-85-6 (Mobipocket)

For Library of Congress Cataloguing-in-Publication Information,
contact the publisher
Printed in the United States by FCI Digital

CONTENTS

PROCEED WITH CAUTION

QUINTAY

THAT DAY WE SAW an ambulance arrive, followed by two new cars. Right away we guessed they were from Santiago. They followed the road that ran alongside the cove and led to the whale processing plant. From the other end of that mouth open to the Pacific, where our houses are, we saw them open the doors and get out of the vehicles. The first thing they did was to lift their hands and cover up their noses and mouths. It's the inevitable, automatic gesture that all new arrivals make. You did it, too; no one escapes that reaction. There were several men and a few women, almost all of them—except for one who wore a dark suit—in white smocks and carrying briefcases and boxes they pulled along in a little wagon.

They moved along the concrete esplanade, till one of the

women in the party stopped short, arched her body forward, and vomited forcefully. The women standing beside her moved away in a reflex action, perhaps out of disgust, perhaps to protect their clothing from stains. Everyone stopped walking, never taking their hands from their faces. One of the men in white came closer and steadied her, placing a hand on the woman's bent back, and with the other offering her a handkerchief that he had taken from the pocket of his smock so that she could clean herself. We couldn't see that man's expression because we were so far away, but we imagined he must have wrinkled his nose when he moved his hand to grab the handkerchief and the smell penetrated all the openings in his face. The woman stood there motionless for a few moments, wiped her face with the handkerchief, which she then balled up and stuck into one of the pockets of her smock. Then she stood up straight and nodded, no doubt to confirm that she was ready to move on. After that we saw them go up the road and along the ramp that leads to the building.

But before I continue, I need to tell you that that stench, which invades everything, isn't the odor of Quintay itself; it arrived much later, with the people from the processing plant. Because Quintay used to be us fishermen with our nets and boats and brightly colored wooden houses at the edge of the cove. And also the whales' tails sticking up high in the distance, which the kids greeted with delight and regarded with admiration, up on the black coastal rocks. Not those who came to work in the processing plant, because none of the townspeople accepted it or wanted any part of it: not the smooth, huge, square buildings or the horrible concrete ramp. That's not Quintay.

Ever since they came, the smell is everywhere, solid, as if the air was congealed grease that you have to dive into and paddle through and climb aboard the boat and go way out to sea, fishing, far from the whaling ships, in search of someplace where you can breathe at last. But, of course, at the end of the day you've got to bring food home for the family, plunge once more into that dense, stinking smell in order to get back home. And, later, seated around the table, burn incense in the heaters so the food won't make you sick to your stomach, because if you don't, there's no way to put anything in your mouth without heaving.

It's just that the smell fouls up everything, and those people are no exception. To tell the truth, they have a worse time of it than we do, because even if they bathe and scrub and perfume themselves, and wash their clothes and hang them out in the sun to dry, when those folks from the processing plant go into town to buy provisions for the month, there's no way the locals from Valparaíso can help screwing up their faces and moving aside, or even whispering softly among themselves, though not softly enough to keep the others from hearing: There go those stinkpots from Quintay.

A thousand arrived, all of them men, and they have their soccer and movies and electric lights, which we don't have, no, none of it. That's why they don't mind the smell too much. And besides, they earn a lot of dough and can invite their friends out for drinks and dinners, and even give gifts to the young ladies from the city, who all at once stop wrinkling their noses and smile. Although deep down, or maybe not so deep down, they know that they go out and drink themselves into a stupor in order to forget the moment when the blood splatters up toward them, covering them completely, a thick blood that runs down their faces, their hands, their clothing, as they hear the piecing cry of the calf who circles nearby, calling for its mother. They drink and laugh at the Social Club and listen to Antonio Prieto sing, and they rest their heads on the girls' shoulders, *Clock, don't tick away the hours*, between many rounds of pisco, *so that dawn will never come*, till they fall off their feet, in an attempt to quell the identical, carbon-copy nightmares they all have—you know?—repeated again and again, till they can't stand it anymore, each and every night.

On their backs they receive the dry blow of harpoon piercing spine; they feel the sharp spurs expand as they plunge into flesh, penetrating deeply; and they feel the container of sulfuric acid open up, allowing the acid to spill out and spread through the entrails, till it makes the grenade on the tip of the damn device explode. And they awaken screaming, soaked in sweat, gasping as if all the air had suddenly escaped from their lungs.

In the daytime, it's always the same for them: they tie the tail of each whale to the boats and drag them out to the buoys. And, as there's no keeping up with the number of captured whales, they fill them with air, inflating and inflating with the compressor so that they'll float, awaiting their turn to be processed the next day, or the day after that. Then the cove fills with floating bodies, illuminated by the moon and rocked by the waves: radiant, luminous death on the surface of the water. Our little ones can't control their curiosity and, when we're not watching they secretly spy, barely pushing aside the thick curtains our wives have hung on the windows to avoid seeing that view all the time.

Later, at dawn, the poor creatures are tied to a steel cable connected to a winch and dragged up the enormous ramp next to the dock, to the butchering platform. Once there, when the pickaxes are sunk into them to begin the processing, a stream of fetid water spurts out, inundating everything. And, even though no one will admit it, believe me, it's as if hell has opened up and you can never be safe again.

They walk, and sometimes they run, those people, the ones from the processing plant, in their cleated shoes, over the tamed, slippery flesh. At certain times it seems like a game that even makes some of them laugh, a bitter laughter that allows you to see the dark holes where their teeth are missing. Because that's what's started happening to them: their teeth have begun to fall out. With no explanation, no cause, you might say.

First it was one man, then another, and another, and yet another. And then there were many, and finally all of them, no matter what their age, physical condition, or job at the plant: from the workers to the bosses. So they brought a doctor from Valparaíso who examined them and prescribed some vitamins, or at least that's what they told us. They all took them religiously, waiting for the misfortune to end. But time went by and everything stayed the same: their teeth kept falling out, resistant to all treatment.

Then that group from Santiago came, arriving with doctors and nurses and syringes, to take samples of everyone's blood. And there was the business of that woman, of course, the one who vomited; I've already told you about that. What I didn't tell you is that the poor thing felt sick all day long, according to what some of them told us later. And suddenly she started shouting things that no one—around there—wanted to hear. There was no way to make her stop, till they got off the ship and went to the cove and climbed into their cars and went away forever.

A few days later the results of the tests and analyses arrived in white, typed envelopes, which the people in charge of the plant read and reread without managing to clear up any of it.

Later they brought in a priest, who came bearing crosses, incense, and holy water. But he didn't get past the entrance; he just made a few movements, right there, beside the diocesan minivan that had brought him, and after a while he returned, fast as could be, to Valparaíso, as white as a sheet of paper, they said. And it was then that some people began to feel afraid. And the fear began circulating among them, like an unstoppable plague.

And they're right, I say. They're absolutely right, don't you agree? That's why they don't talk, you know? They won't tell you a thing. We, on the other hand, the ones from Quintay, those who always, for generations, have lived in Quintay, we're not afraid: we're disgusted and sad. And we've got all our teeth. Waiting for the nightmare to end one day and for us to be able to pull down the curtains, open the windows and doors, go outside to watch the sea from the black rocks of the cove. And to smile again, of course, without covering our mouths with our hands, like they do.

BLACK DOG

IT'S DARK NOW: that's how it is in winter. Before you know it, it's six o'clock and already nighttime. I hear the noise of an engine and brakes squealing, just as I turn off the light so they won't see me, and I tiptoe over to the front window. A door slams; luckily I didn't close the blinds. I just need to pull the curtain aside a little in order to see. There's a Jeep: it doesn't belong to any of the locals because around here we all know one another. A girl gets out; you can tell she's from Buenos Aires by that ankle-length skirt she's wearing and her long, loose hair, like a hippie. In that outfit, and with the handful of pesos she probably has on her, what could she expect to find but the Fabbianis' upstairs room, which, since Gina died, is turning into a tenement. The house is empty now because there was a problem with the water pipes, and the downstairs rooms were left a shambles. No doubt they'll be that way for a long time because Gina's kids don't take care of them.

Directly below the mercury lamp, the girl opens the door to the tailgate of the Jeep and takes out a suitcase, which can't be holding too much because you can tell it's light. A black bulk stands up at the back of the tailgate: it's an enormous dog, whose size—my God!—is enough to scare a person, even from far away. The girl motions to him and the beast jumps out and stands next to her. The driver doesn't bother to get out; as soon as he sees them on the sidewalk he hits the gas and takes off. She looks one way and another, like someone who's afraid or has something to hide, though who would be afraid with that dog for protection. She goes over to the front door, rests the suitcase on the step, and after rummaging in her woven purse for a while, pulls out a key. So: it seems she has a key. She must've stopped by Gina's kids' house first; if not, how could she have gotten it. I know that house: old, and lovely in its day, with two stories and the terrace. When Gina used to visit her daughter in Buenos Aires, because poor Gina (may God keep her in His glory) has—or had—two boys here and her girl in Buenos Aires; the daughter went there to study and never came back, as if she had turned her back on the city where she was born ... well, the thing is, whenever Gina went to the capital, she'd leave me the key so I could water the plants. She kept the house immaculate, floors shiny, not a speck of dust on the furniture, with those lovely crocheted doilies and those little porcelain figurines. Now everything is dark, a disaster, ever since the business with the pipes, except for the fact that a few days ago Rubén managed to get the lights working on the upstairs level. The girl walks in; she might be one of Gina's daughter's friends, I suppose. She walks in with

the dog and the suitcase and for a while it's as if the darkness
has swallowed her up. Of course it'll take her a while to cross
the vestibule and the living room, climb the staircase and
find the light switch for the upstairs room. She should have
brought a flashlight, but, then again, if they don't tell her, how
is she supposed to know. Since it's cold, while I'm waiting I
decide to feel my way into the kitchen to make myself some
tea. I don't want to turn on the light in the living room in case
the girl is right there, watching; I wonder if she'll get the idea
to come over and ask for something. Whenever I go over to
bring Father Renato something to eat or to arrange the flowers
at church, he tells me to be careful, things are happening; I
don't know what things, but just to be on the safe side I listen
to him and watch out for myself. I take the big blue cup out of
the cupboard, pop in the teabag, two teaspoons of sugar, the
water's boiling, I stir, I leave the spoon on the counter, turn
off the kitchen light, and walk through the hallway and the
living room, taking care not to trip over anything. I place the
cup on the counter beside the statue of the Blessed Virgin, on
the piece of furniture next to the window. With the sliver of
light coming in from the street I see Her kind, protecting eyes.
I open the curtain a little and get a slight shock, because the
movement I make coincides exactly with the light that goes on
in the room across the street. It's a bare window, no curtains,
blinds, or shutters, so I can see pretty well: the girl is sitting at
the foot of a large bed, her suitcase on the floor, the dog beside
her. Suddenly she grabs her head and bends over her knees; it
looks like she's crying. The dog rests one paw on her lap. And
I take a sip of tea, to shake off this cold that's gotten into my
body and makes me tremble.

You don't see her much during the day. Sometimes she walks the dog over to Olga's, around the corner from here, to buy something to eat. Esther told me that Aldo offered her the bones and leftover pieces of meat from the butcher shop. Sure, I say, considering what a slimeball Aldo is, and her a young hippie girl! The other day Aldo showed up and rang my bell; he was carrying a package wrapped in newspaper and he explained to me that he had been there I don't know how long, banging on the door across the way—because like everyone else, he knows that the bell hasn't worked since that business with the pipes—but that the girl hadn't answered. He asked if he could leave the bones for the dog with me, so that I could give them to her when she got home. I told him I never saw her, that he should leave the package at the door and she'd find it. He stood there staring at me without a word; then he turned around, as if to cross the street, looked at me again, and finally made up his mind to cross. I shut the door and opened the peephole to see what he was doing. He took a piece of string from his pocket, wrapped it around the package a few times and left it tied to the doorknob, no doubt to keep some random mutt from coming along and taking the meat, and I say meat because the package looked soft—and he doesn't fool me by saying it was only bones, no way!

It's late when I'm awakened by the engine noise I think I recognize; I put on my slippers and walk to the living room. Hidden behind the curtain, I see through the cracks in the shutters the same Jeep as last time; it barely stops. The light in the front room goes on, someone gets out of the vehicle, it looks like a boy with a bundle over his shoulder, but everything happens quickly and the damn shutters don't let me see too clearly: the Jeep goes away, Gina's door swings open, the guy walks in, the door closes. By the time I raise my head, they're already upstairs hugging and ripping their clothes off; the dog watches them, wagging his tail; then both of them fall into bed. I see everything cut off in slices of light and shadow, but in spite of all that, I'm sure he sticks his tongue in her mouth and runs his hands over her tits. Then the black dog, as if he's heard or seen something, walks over to the window of the room and looks in my direction. I'm frozen, my eyes glued to the animal's, and I start to feel dizzy, like short of breath. I hold on to the wall and drag myself as best I can over to the little flowered chair to sit down. A band of mercury light filters in through the opening left by the half-drawn curtain, tracing a sharp, vertical white stripe over the statue of the Virgin that stands on top of the furniture. I see a tear roll down Her cheek. I'm sorry, Blessed Mother, I whisper. I'm sorry.

I'm inserting the key in the lock of the front door, back home after bringing Father Renato the washed and ironed altar cloths, when I hear voices coming from behind me. I sneak a glance over my shoulder and see Aldo approaching along the sidewalk in front, after greeting Don Mario, who passed by on his bike. Now Aldo stops and bangs on the hippie's door, with a new package, it seems. He turns and greets me, what a nuisance. Oh, Aldo, I haven't seen her, I tell him, pretending to look for something in my purse. Suddenly the door opens and the girl peers out. You can tell she's taken the package because she stretches out her hand and grabs it, I hear her thank him, and Aldo doesn't let go of it, and she pulls it a little towards herself, and he crawls his hand over the package like a spider so he can touch her hand, which she withdraws suddenly. Aldo is so startled that he lets go, too. Then, plop! the package falls noisily to the sidewalk, the paper rips open, and the bones and steaks scatter. He bends to pick them up and tries to touch her leg, but she pulls back and slams the door. I quickly turn toward my door, twist the key and open up, as I hear, first: *Dirty whore!* And then Aldo's angry footsteps retreating.

I light a candle to the statue of Jesus on the dresser in my room and I refill the little vase that always stands beside it with some chrysanthemums from Esther's garden. We're having *mate* today because she's a big *mate* fan, even though afterward it gives me heartburn, but all right, *mate* loosens the tongue, stimulates conversation, and so I've got to put up with it if I want to find out anything. The thing is, whenever I mention it, Esther doesn't seem to know that there's a guy living at the hippie's place. So I tell her what went on when he arrived. The part about them naked in bed I don't tell her, but I do say that he has a beard, long hair, and that he showed up with nothing but a little bag. And Esther says to me that if a guy had been there she would've seen him. *I* saw, I reply, or isn't that enough for you? Are you sure? the damn fool goes, as if I made it up, as if I didn't know what I saw with my own eyes. Of course it was nighttime, of course he might have left a few hours earlier and not been there anymore, but I'm sure the guy's still there, though when the light is on I don't see him; he must be hiding. Are you saying they're . . .? Esther interrupts. I shrug and can't come up with an answer. Because if that's the case, she hints, stretching out her arm with another overflowing *mate*, which I don't know how she's going to be able to swallow, we'll have to tell someone. Father Renato? I ask. Or the chief of police, she whispers, as though she was afraid we'd be overheard. I stand there in front of the statue of Jesus, with my hands still wrapped around the chrysanthemums I've just arranged, and suddenly it occurs to me that He has the same burning eyes as the dog.

I've been watching for a few nights now but I don't see the guy. He must be staying downstairs, in the empty part of the house. Since the hippie never opens the front windows, you can't see anything. At night I imagine he goes upstairs to the room when she turns out the light. They must eat in the kitchen, with a candle. That kitchen has to be filthy by now because without water ... and besides, I don't think the hippie is crazy about cleaning. I don't even want to think about what condition everything must be in. If Gina saw the house, the poor thing would die all over again. Today, while I'm busy watching, I've brought along my late mother's rosary, the one that was blessed by Pope Paul VI; I've got it rolled up in my hands so it will protect me from that dog.

It seems I fell asleep and got a cramp in my leg. I rub it a little with my hand, and then I lift my head: the lights are on in the room across the way. That filthy pig—naked again—is touching herself down there; the dog stares at her with his tongue hanging out. She bends her legs and keeps on touching herself. The dog has placed his two front paws on the bed and watches her from closer up. The guy sees it all; I know because his profile is projected in shadows above the hippie's body; no doubt they're going to roll around in the bed. But now, suddenly, she stands, as if something startled her, and covers herself with the sheet. I quickly duck my head and hide behind the curtain. Oops, I forgot to snuff the candle that I lit to the Virgin earlier today. I crawl along the floor, stand up next to the furniture, wet my fingers with saliva, put out the flame, and return to my post by the window. The hippie is on all fours, like a bitch, and the black dog goes over to her and runs his tongue along her ass crack. She arches her back, stretches, doubles over; you can tell they like it—both her and the guy who's watching. And the dog, too, though suddenly he pounces on the windowsill and barks furiously. The shock knocks me against the frozen wall, until I slip down onto the floor and there I stay, looking at the crystal beads of Mama's rosary digging into the flesh of my hands.

The hippie comes back, from Olga's place most likely, because she's carrying a basket with some leeks, celery, and green onions sticking out. You can see the surprise on her face when she finds the package hanging from the doorknob. She looks one way, then the other, and just as she begins to untie it, the black beast, who had been peeing against the neighbor's tree, hurls himself at the package, which ends up falling, in a flash rips open the newspaper wrapping with his paws, gulps down a dense lump of chopped meat in two bites and runs off toward the corner with some marrow in his maw. Angrily she yells something at him, but then she gestures with her head, smiles, opens the door, and goes inside. At that very moment a wind comes up, sweeping away the shreds of paper now scattered along the sidewalk. And I decide to head for the patio to collect the clothes I have hanging on the line, so that they won't get all covered with dirt.

I'm startled awake by banging on my door. I glance at the clock: it's nearly 3 AM. The desperate banging resumes, now accompanied by repeated shouts: Please! Please, open up! I slip on a robe and run to the front door. Through the peephole I see the hippie, half-dressed and with her hair all disheveled. I open the little window above the door. There's something wrong with my dog; he's very sick, she says, nervously, sniffling. He's acting like he's been poisoned or something. Where can I take him? Is there a veterinarian in the neighborhood? Jiménez, I reply, and sticking my hand through the window a little, I point to the right. Two blocks away, I add, but at this time of night ... She doesn't say a thing, but turns rapidly and runs across the street. I close the little window, but not all the way, and stand there watching through a crack. She opens the door, goes inside and comes back out right away. She's put on a coat and a woolen cap. She struggles along with the dog in her arms; it's obvious that the animal is as heavy as a corpse. No sign of the guy. I remain there watching till she disappears. I go to the kitchen for a glass of water and realize that I've left that huge mess I made earlier and never cleaned up. What was I thinking! I grumble, as I put away the hammer, shake out the old rag and very carefully begin to clean. On the countertop there's still lots of fine dust, the mouth of the bottle, and some shards of rosary crystal. I remove the little chain from the remains of the broken beads and hang it around my neck; the cross hasn't been damaged and is still beautiful. I wrap the debris in newspaper, moisten it with the holy water I brought home from church in a jar, and leave them in a corner. Tomorrow I'll give it all a proper burial.

I hear the squeal of brakes, the noise of an engine, but this time I'm sure it's not the Jeep. I also hear some shouts. I tiptoe over to the window. For several nights now I haven't closed the shutters all the way; I always leave one panel open. There's a gray car at the door of Gina's house, and now the van from the police station arrives and parks. A couple of guys get out of the gray car and kick down the front door of the house; one of them pulls the hippie, handcuffed, from the car and drags her along with him. She turns over and shouts toward the streets with all her strength: Aldo, you son of a bitch! Esther, I think. The guy who's dragging the girl slaps her in the face and pushes her inside. The lights of the house next door flash on and rapidly flash off again. Father Renato told me it's better not to see anything, or else you're the one who'll end up with problems. The cops stay outside with their weapons drawn; not a soul on the street, and you can tell that it's nearly daybreak because I can hear Vilma's rooster crowing. Her chicken coop is next to my patio.

I can't sleep with this fire I have in my gut, and no matter how much bicarbonate I take, I can't get any relief. And as if that wasn't enough, that dog's eyes haunt me, also his barking, sometimes during the day, other times at night. Even though Esther said that Jiménez told her he couldn't have done anything to save him, I can still hear him barking at me from the room across the way. I see him, too. And besides, there are those voices, although the house is empty, though everyone reassures me again and again that it's all over. Even though Father Renato has comforted me, telling me that the Virgin I have in the living room is very old, and that these pieces have their secrets, especially when they're so old, and that wood is alive, of course; that's why it's not unusual that it's developed a crack. But I know that Her face split open there, right where the white light from the street hit Her that night. And I also know that it's there Her cries come from, Her icy moans.

THE GUEST

I'M OUT HERE on the balcony now, but I can see her anyway, through the sliding glass door. She comes and goes, from the tiny kitchen of the apartment to the living-dining room. She has spread out and painstakingly adjusted the floral tablecloth that she uses for special occasions, and now she passes by carrying four glasses that she deposits on the table, although from what she said earlier, there will be only two of them, the guest and her. It's just that she likes everything to be completely separate: wine on one side, water on the other; meat over here, vegetables over there; a little plate for bread, another for toast. Well, everyone's got their obsessions, and hers are pretty harmless. As for me, I'm a simpler creature, I'm not usually so particular.

I look outside and entertain myself watching the neighbor, who steps out onto the balcony of the building across the way. She leans forward, making a sign to someone who is obviously down on the sidewalk but who I can't see from here, drops something that looks like a bundle of keys tied to a blue ribbon, and when the ribbon is extended, she lets go of the other end. She adjusts her hair, goes inside, closes the sliding door, and suddenly I can see myself—I've always had very good vision—reflected beside the flowerpots on our balcony; she, on the other hand, has been swallowed up by the darkness indoors. Now a floor lamp lights up, no doubt she turned it on as she walked to the door, where she's probably greeting the person she's been waiting for, someone she likes, I imagine, and has been anxiously awaiting.

I turn my attention to the inside of our apartment: she goes by with two bread baskets, just as I expected—one with bread, the other with toast. She deposits them in the middle of the table and disappears from view when she returns to the kitchen. I stay here looking at the slightly sad leaves on the ficus plant that stands in the corner of the balcony; I imagine they need water. I turn toward the sky, it's dark already, the street lights have switched on, hardly any stars and no moon at all; maybe a storm is brewing. Inside, she comes back into view, carrying two small, overfull bowls—that's why I can see what's peeking out—one holding a yellow dip, and the other a white dip with green specks. It's for spreading on the bread while they talk and wait for the warm main meal to be ready. Juancu, the boyfriend she broke up with not long ago (I don't know why, because he was really cool and I liked him a lot), loved the white dip with green specks, which he ate with breadsticks; he always asked her to make it. When the mixture was ready, he would take it to the sofa where sometimes all three of us, together, would watch those National Geographic shows that I find so fascinating, and we'd eat there happily and have so much fun.

What I regret most about tonight's date is that I won't be able to watch the jungle program they're showing later. But of course it's understandable; in cases like this, when the guest is coming over for the first time, it's better for them to be alone. She glances at her cell phone, puts her hand on her head, and goes running toward the bedroom, the only one in the apartment. For the time being I remain staring out; I enjoy being on the balcony.

You can tell the traffic must be heavy because you can hear horns honking and even a *motherfucker* now rising in a hoarse, deep voice. I've always wanted to have a deep voice because it sounds more macho, but, well, over time you learn to accept whatever fate deals you. A pigeon goes by, flying very close, maybe, I think, with the intention of sticking around, but at last he passes out of view. I don't like pigeons; they're so gray, and besides, they disgust me a little because they make everything dirty. Just as well it kept going.

She returns in a long red dress that looks very nice on her. Hmmm, red—you can see that she's chosen her very finest for this meeting. She stands in front of the mirror on the other side of the sofa, near the table, paints her lips (also red), combs her hair, goes back to the bedroom. I like that mirror; sometimes I stand there for a long time looking at myself in it. She brought it home from an auction one day because her mother had told her that mirrors make spaces look bigger. She's back, taller now, in a pair of black sandals she wears very often, but which still

27

look like new because they're so uncomfortable that she ends up taking them off and walking around the house barefoot. She's very natural: when she's home alone, that's when I think she's prettiest. In fact, I tell her so whenever I can.

She heads for the kitchen, no doubt to see how everything is coming along. You can hear the sound the oven door makes; it's a terrible squawk, like a crow's. The noise of that door gives me goosebumps; sometimes I try to make her understand, but she shrugs and wrinkles her brow as though she can't hear me, or maybe she just doesn't take it too seriously. Then I tell her again that she looks very pretty like that, natural and at home, and she gives me another smile.

The doorbell rings, she crosses the room quickly but stops short and turns around, stops in front of the mirror, checks her appearance, fixes her hair once more and takes off again. She reaches the door. I can hear her open it: a *hi*, another *hi*, the soft pop of a kiss, a few steps, more steps, and now I can see him, he's got two liter-size bottles of beer in his hand, so I imagine he probably doesn't like wine. What a shame, because she appreciates good wine, especially if it's a Cabernet Sauvignon, I've heard her say so many times, and Juancu always brought her some. That Juancu was a great guy.

He's sitting now, he's taken a cell phone out of his pocket, and while he touches the screen and places it on the table, he starts looking all around the place curiously, stretching his body so he can see better, taking advantage of the fact that she had to go back to the kitchen, probably to stick one of the beers in the fridge so it won't get warm, because warm beer is like cat piss; that's what Aunt Lucrecia always used to say, and you can tell it's become engraved in my memory. The other bottle was left behind, between the bread baskets, and it's sweating cold drops. A little bell dings, no doubt an alert from WhatsApp or Twitter or Facebook. She lives on her phone, too; that's why I'm so up on all of that. He grabs his cell phone again, touches the screen, smiles.

She walks in carrying a mug for the beer, just one. You can tell she's decided just to drink wine. He puts the cell phone aside, she picks up the two glasses she had brought for the wine and her guest's water and disappears behind the kitchen door. Another little ding and he types something, presses his finger against the screen again, and stares intently. *Anything new?* she asks him as she prepares to leave the room again. *No, nothing, just Facu's stupid jokes because Boca lost, and another dumb gag from that pain in the ass, Albertina.* She comes back with an opener for the beer, pries off the top, he types something again, she sits, they look at one another, he smears a slice of bread with the yellow dip, she, a piece of toast with the green-and-white stuff. *Nice apartment,* he remarks. *Yes, it belonged to my aunt; it's small, but it's fine for me, and besides, the neighborhood ...* And just then, wouldn't you know it, the garbage truck rolls by, making an infernal noise; that's what the next-door neighbor always says, she goes out on the balcony, complains, leans over toward the street and curses, though with that noise nobody will hear her except me, because I've got very keen hearing and I'm usually on the balcony at this time of day, just for a little while before that National Geographic jungle program comes on, which I'm sure to miss tonight. But the neighbor doesn't come out on the balcony to curse, how strange, maybe she isn't home. I return to the scene of the date and see that she, too, is fiddling with her cell phone, that huge, flat one of hers, which looks like a cutting board for dicing onions, she types away at full speed and with all her fingers; you've got to admit she's got a talent for these things ... They eat: another slice of bread for him, another piece of toast for her. They take a few sips: beer for him, wine for her. Suddenly she pops up, goes to the kitchen and comes back right away, holding a plate with two juicy melon wedges with ham. He says he'll have the ham, but he doesn't like melon; she helps herself to the melon he's put aside. *May I?* he asks, serving himself the other slice of ham. *Yes*, she replies, *of course*. The other melon wedge is still there, abandoned on the plate. With me it's just the opposite: I like melon, in fact I love it, but not ham. It's not that I don't like it, but it's very salty and makes me sick; that's why she doesn't let me eat it. Aunt Lucrecia always used to say: *Raw ham is awful, it leaves your mouth as dry as a parrot's tongue.* And she repeated it so often that it's impossible for me to forget.

The two of them carry on like before, typing away on their cell phones, and every so often a mouthful, a sip, a smile. Now she gets up, takes his plate—he's eaten all the slices of ham—places it on top of hers, then the one with the melon slice on top of the other two, collects the used utensils and goes to the kitchen. He's still nailed to the chair, forget about helping her, Juancu, now that guy *did* help, he even cooked sometimes. She comes in with a lovely little white porcelain dish, with a cover, all decorated with green leaves, like vines, raised and intertwined, which she carries in a wooden holder. She sets the whole thing on the table, lifts the lid, and dense steam rises in the air. *Ham and cheese cannelloni for you, and vegetable cannelloni for me*, she says, standing there and staring at it. *Ham and cheese cannelloni!* he repeats with a certain amount of enthusiasm, *How did you know? Facu told me on*

WhatsApp yesterday when he found out you were coming over.
She leans over to start serving it, but he stops her: *Stop, stop,
everybody needs to see this.* He stands, extends one arm, takes
a snapshot of the cannelloni on the dish. I barely manage to
see a white flash explode, that light always makes me nervous,
it's even worse when it hits me in the face, but that's not this
time because I'm not too close, and the beam of light vanishes
before it can affect me. He goes on typing; sometimes it seems
like he's inside the cell phone. She looks at hers. *They look very
good in the picture,* she says to him; *thanks for what you put in
your tweet, also.* He keeps typing, she stands, serves him two
cannelloni, then takes another two for herself. The casserole
dish is still steaming; there must be more left. She replaces the
cover. I like the vegetable ones; hers come out really delicious.
He scoops up a big serving of cannelloni with his fork and
suspends it for a moment over his open mouth as he stares
intently at the cell phone. The cheese drips onto the plate. Then
she quickly sticks out her hand with the device and clicks. He
opens his mouth, swallows, smiles, she eats a small portion
while she touches the screen and types. She continues staring,
takes another bite. He does the same. *I look like an idiot,* he
says, seeing himself in the photo that just now appears on his
screen, and he laughs.

He helps himself to more beer; you've got to admit that
at least he shows some initiative for that. He leaves the now-
empty bottle on the table. She serves herself wine, picks up
the large glass and brings it to her lips. He extends his arm
with the cell phone, she assumes a seductive pose, smiles, he
clicks, and once more the flash. He types away and presses
the screen, then it's her turn, looking at her own cell phone:
Oh, thanks, you wrote that I'm very pretty. He nods, unable to

speak because his mouth is once again filled with ham and cheese cannelloni, and besides you can tell he's not much of a talker. She swallows a few times and then takes an extreme close-up shot of the wine bottle, now half-empty. Then she types, touches the screen, smiles. He looks at his cell phone, makes a face, takes a close-up photo of his half-empty beer mug, and does the same. She glances at her screen, *Oh*, she says, *bummer about the wine*. They eat and drink in a silence occasionally interrupted by all sorts of message alerts: dings, whistles, froggy croaks. She serves him another cannelloni, crossing the utensils on top of her empty plate. The thing is, melon is more filling than ham, and, besides, she watches her weight; that's why she has such an amazing figure, which this stupid jerk doesn't even look at.

With Juancu there were times when they hadn't even finished eating and one of them would say something, or else they just looked at each other, and then they'd get up, automatically, embrace, and without peeling apart they would stumble around, lips locked, ripping off their clothes and falling onto the sofa. Someone phones, he gets up, answers, walks from the table to the door, back and forth, talking very loud: football jokes, lots of *asshole*, lots of *everything's cool*. She picks up the plates, goes to the kitchen, returns, collects the casserole dish. He hangs up. *It's Facu, he's such a drag. He says hi. Ah*, she says, carrying the casserole to the kitchen. You can hear the noise of things being piled up on the countertop, others deposited in the sink. He sits down again, wipes his mouth with the napkin. She arrives with two little plates holding ice cream bonbons, with a spoon on each one. She hands one to him, placing hers next to the half-empty glass of wine. He drinks the beer remaining in his glass in a single gulp; she can see that there's no more left in the bottle. She picks it up and heads back toward the kitchen. You can hear footsteps, the refrigerator door.

Then he stands up, the little plate in his hand, and walks toward the sofa. Well, at least that's something, and now I can see him much closer up, though only from the back; he's got a nice back. He leaves the little plate of ice cream on the coffee table. *Oh, there you are*, she says, startled, when she emerges. He gets up, grabs the bottle and picks up his beer mug, places all of it on the coffee table, and sits. She brings over her little plate with the ice cream and her cell phone, turns toward the dining table to get her glass of wine, fills it before picking it up, walks over with a smile, leaving everything on the coffee table. They take a photo of the little table, both of them at once; luckily the flash burst is on the other side. They type, smile, type, touch. Then he leans toward her, gives her a kiss, she allows herself to be kissed, they embrace without letting go of their cell phones, moving like octopi, their tentacles flapping, and then there's an unintentional click and a bright blaze strikes me right in the eyes, and then another click and another blaze. At that moment I feel like I've had enough, like I can't keep quiet anymore. *Potato for Ernesto!* I screech, with all the vocal resources at my disposal, *potato for Ernesto!*

What's that? he asks, startled, turning toward the sliding glass door that leads to the balcony. *Ernesto*, she says, resigned, looking at me with irritation and wrinkling her brow. *Natural and at home, prettier*, I say, trying to drive away her annoyance and make her smile at me. He stands up immediately and comes over, opens the sliding door, and takes a picture of me— with the flash. *No! Don't do that, it makes him really nervous*, she shouts. *Oh, ha-ha, the little bugger has a personality*, he mocks as he types. *Asshole, asshole!* I scream into his face. *Oh, so that's how it is?* the asshole says. And when he threatens to take another photo, I turn my back to him. The night has grown darker; a lightning bolt crosses the sky. The neighbor across the way is sitting next to her guest on an outdoor sofa they keep on the balcony. With glasses in their hands, they converse, look at one another.

Now her voice, very near, takes me by surprise; you can tell she's pushed that jerk aside because her soft steps are growing closer. *Bedtime, Ernesto,* she says to me, and she comes closer with the cloth. *Natural and at home, prettier,* I say. *Bedtime,* she insists, *come on.* She smiles. She covers the cage. I fall silent. The footsteps fade, I hear the click of the sliding glass door as it closes. The cloth is opaque, but I can still distinguish the sparks of a new flash of lightning anyway. The noise of glasses in the kitchen. I hope that asshole goes away before it starts pouring, I think, or I'll get drenched for a lost cause.

Suddenly, once more, the click of the door. A hand lifts the cloth, yanks it off, throws it to the ground; the asshole's face, which has surrounded the cage, faces me and flash, flash, flash. I close my eyes and screech in his face: *Mmmm, Juancu fucks me so niiice! Mmmm, Juancu fucks me so niiice!,* my phrase is pure vibrato as I repeat it, blindly, while I shift the weight of my body from one foot to another in a rocking motion that makes my voice flow more powerfully. He stops short, quits taking photos; she hurries over quickly, tells him to go home, that it's enough, as she pushes him toward the door. They struggle; I worry. *Asshole, asshole!* I scream. *So Juancu fucks you better?* he charges, unhinged. She doesn't answer, grabs the cell phone, takes his picture. *You're horrible,* she shouts at him, touches the screen, types. *Ha-ha-ha, look who's talking, the poor dumped girlfriend*, he says with devastating rage. *Asshole, asshole!* I persist from my position.

At last he leaves, slamming the door behind him. She stands there frozen for a moment, suspended I-don't-know-where. Then, as if awakening, she starts pacing back and forth, angrily, tearfully, from the table to the kitchen. I hear the clatter of the dishes against the sink, the utensils falling on the floor, drawers opening and closing. The friction of the tablecloth as it rubs together. And soon, nothing.

She emerges from the kitchen, grabs the door frame, leans over, takes off one sandal, looks at me, hurls it at the sofa; then the other, which she throws even farther, hitting the bedroom door. *Prettier!* I screech. Then she retraces her steps, goes into the kitchen, comes out one minute later, walks toward me with a little plate holding a piece of vegetable cannelloni, opens the cage. *Come on*, she says to me, as she sticks in her free hand. I jump up on the extended finger, we walk to the living room, she sits on the sofa, puts the little plate on the coffee table, I jump onto the table. *Potato for Ernesto*, I say; I lean over and eat. Behind us you can hear the first raindrops falling. She grabs the remote control that was behind one of the cushions and turns on the TV. The National Geographic program fills the screen. She lifts the skirt of her red dress to dry her eyes. On the little plates the ice cream bonbons have started to melt.

CHINESE BOY

HE SITS DOWN on the same park bench, but at the other end. He's so incredibly thin that I can't help glancing at him quickly, fleetingly: the long, endless legs, which he now bends and crosses, one over the other; his eyes nailed so firmly to his sneakers that I can't quite see them. His deep black hair, almost blue, covers up most of his face. As if she knows I'm concentrating on something else, Lavender struggles uncomfortably; she wants to get down from my lap. I leave her on the grass, adjusting the barrettes I put in her bangs to lift them into two stylish topknots; I unhook the leash from her collar and let her run. I have issues with the Chinese; they make me feel uneasy, but not all of them—that is, the Chinese who live in China seem all right, but those who live here don't, what can I say, maybe they make me think of the Chinese supermarkets where people say they turn off the refrigerators at night to save money, and the next day they sell you spoiled dairy and rotten meat. As soon as I set her loose, Lavender starts running around the bench hysterically. No matter how much room she has, she always does the same thing, as if she doesn't understand she's not on leash anymore. I also think about the Chinese mafia, their secret workshops, fake credit cards, white slavery. After a couple of revolutions around this tiny planetary system, Lavender slows up and stops right in front of me, to make sure I'm still here, I suppose, because with so much spinning and spinning, the world looks a little different to her and it's not so easy for her to figure things out. I rub my hand over the little curls on her back, and then I look at the Chinese boy and he looks at me: *Behave yourself,* I tell her. I know her intentions; she takes a few nervous, tiny steps toward the other end of the bench. *Lavender, stop bothering people,* I warn her. Chinese Boy understands that he's the people in question and then he looks at Lavender and at me with eyes so slanted that I wonder how everything must look through such narrowness. *No bother, no worry,* he says, smiling, while I go on thinking about Chinese people and Chinese restaurants that serve dog meat. Lavender sniffs his sneakers, and then I can't help seeing him snatch her and run away with her, her piercing, desperate, pathetic barks, the boy's stride so wide that he seems to move without touching the floor, and me with these platform heels and this purse and the leash hanging from my arm, which I clumsily drag along the ground. And yet Chinese Boy is still sitting there on the other end of the bench; he motions with his hand as if to reassure me that everything's all right—or could it have been to summon an accomplice? Again I think about the Chinese mafia and also, for some odd reason, about gunpowder and fireworks. I call Lavender; she jumps onto my lap. To welcome the New Year, the mayor organized a fireworks display in this park that ended up setting it ablaze. I hook the leash to Lavender's collar and stand up. Chinese Boy looks at us, makes a gesture with his head that I interpret as a goodbye; I attempt a slightly forced smile, as if to conceal my discomfort. Once more he nails his gaze to his sneakers.

I'm drying my hair because I don't like to go out with a wet head. On the dryer I read: *Remington, Made in China*. I'd never paid attention to these details, but now, suddenly, I wonder how many Chinese things there might be in my life. With determination and suspicion, I pick up the bowl that holds the toothpaste and my toothbrush and read: *Origin China*. I look at the bath mat, also Chinese, the little tweezer, the nail file, the hairbrush. My day becomes a yellow quest, a seemingly endless series of turning over this and that. The desk phone, the electric teakettle, the Teflon frying pan, the cup for my breakfast coffee, the netbook cover, my pen drive, the pencil case, the calculator, the case for my glasses, Lavender's barrettes and feeding dish, the pink teddy bear I keep on my bed, the bulb from my bed lamp. And the Italian silk shirt, too?

From a distance, Chinese Boy breaks into my field of vision; I can tell it's him because his height, skinniness, and long, blue-black hair form an unmistakable silhouette; he treads lightly, eyes down, and carries a leash attached to a pet I can't quite make out. Better stop looking, I tell myself, or he'll think I'm waiting for him, and besides, maybe he's not coming this way, what with all the benches there are in the park. Lavender is uneasy; I think she's recognized him and wants to jump down, but I don't let her; what if Chinese Boy's Chinese dog tries to bite her or something worse ... and with all the care I give her! I pull out my cell phone and start checking messages, so as to focus on something else. I don't see him, but I sense him approaching; he veers a little toward my right and at last sits down at the other end of the bench. Lavender is tense, probably because of the nearness of another dog, and since I feel it's rude, even suspicious, to avoid him, I look his way. His legs are crossed, the right ankle resting on his left calf, and then he jerks the leash upward, making the other end pop up behind him, revealing ... a cabbage! Lavender lets out a sharp, brief bark; I can't conceal the surprise stamped on my face like a slap: a pet cabbage! I smile nervously; I had considered the possibility of a Chinese mafioso, a supermarket crook, and even a dog kidnapper, but not a Chinese maniac. I'm starting to get up when I hear him say: *In China work vegetable to meet people.* I stand there frozen, not knowing what to do or say, till I manage to stammer *Work vegetable?* accompanying the question with a hand gesture intended to imitate digging. I remain there looking at him; he laughs, points to the leash attached to the cabbage, stands and walks, the cabbage trailing behind like a dog. Lavender follows his movements closely; Chinese Boy makes a tight turn, walking in circles. *Work?* he asks; I think I understand him and venture: *Walk?* He nods. *Walk*, he confirms, *in China walk vegetable to meet people*, he repeats while sitting back down at the other end of the bench. I respond with an idiotic, dutiful smile, because despite the correction I still don't understand.

Take away negative thought, he explains, as he makes hand gestures for shooing flies or ghosts. *Bad all gone, bad all gone*, he insists, in a voice I now find very pleasant. *Ah*, is all that my state of surprise allows me to express at the moment, vacillating between images of a Chinese mystic or madman, or possibly both. In a moment of carelessness, Lavender jumps down from my lap and, with a combination of curiosity and vigilance, approaches the cabbage that still lies on the ground, tied to the end of the leash beside the boy's feet. *Vegetable not bark or fight with other vegetable*, he laughs. I shrug, smile. *Yes*, I say, *of course*, and suddenly click, I think I'm beginning to understand and think that when a person walks a pet, someone always comes along and asks a question or makes some remark, and having an animal can be useful for meeting people, but—a cabbage? *Are there many people in China who go out walking cabbages?* I ask him. He gestures for me to wait a moment, sticks his hand in his pocket, I stiffen, already on alert, he takes out his cell phone, slides a little closer, toward the middle of the bench, he seems harmless, he shows me a photo, it's a bunch of young people leading cabbages and escarole with leashes and collars, like a meeting of Chihuahua lovers, though considering the Chinese-ness of this tangle, it might be more appropriate to think in terms of Pekingese, Chow Chows, Shar Peis, or something like that. Now he shows me another photo; it looks like him, a couple of years younger, with another Chinese boy; each one leading a cabbage by its leash. *Ah*, I repeat as I seize the opportunity to look at him, the Chinese skin absolutely smooth, perfect; he smiles, I smile. *Let go*, he says to me, pointing to Lavender and the cabbage. I don't know why I agree, but I do: I release Lavender and he lets go of the cabbage, giving it a little push; it rolls, imperfectly, charmingly; Lavender scampers around the cabbage, pushing it with her nose. I look at the Chinese boy to see if it bothers him, he laughs, gestures with his hand as if to say everything's all right. Lavender runs, pushes the cabbage, rolls around in the grass, then rubs against the cabbage, she's going to look like shit, I scold myself, as I imagine the Chinese boy naked, all that Chinese skin against a black silk sheet, and as I can't understand why I'm thinking this, I simply peek at my wristwatch, feign an unexpected emergency, and all at once it's a pretend Oh-I'm-going-to-be-late, a sudden rising from the bench, calling Lavender, attaching her leash and saying goodbye. *Lavender?* the Chinese Boy asks, standing up to look for his cabbage a few steps away. *What means Lavender?* he completes his question, looking at me from over there. *An aromatic plant*, I reply; *it has little, lilac-colored flowers and a beautiful fragrance*, I explain as I pick up my dog, who now smells of cabbage. *Well, I'm off*, I say to the Chinese Boy, leaping into action. *Come back*, I hear him say, *come back tomorrow*, but I don't dare turn around, let alone respond.

A strange new fad has erupted in China: taking vegetables for walks in the street. The leaders of this new fashion are teenagers, who drag vegetables, preferably cabbages, along the sidewalks, pretending they're pets. "They don't bark, fight, or make messes," the kids argue jokingly, but one of their real objectives is to overcome the depression and loneliness that grow along with socioeconomic demands made by the system. I read this on the Internet as I sniff Lavender, who stinks disgustingly, and I curse the Chinese Boy and call the groomer, requesting an urgent appointment. In the process I find out how much it would cost me to tint her curly ears and her frilly topknot lavender or lilac, like I once saw in a poodle magazine. My cell phone beeps, a message from Gastón. I don't answer. I stare at the device: it's made in China, too.

Chinese Boy arrives today with his cabbage and a nosegay of jasmine. No sooner does he sit down than he asks me: *Lavender?* Lavender rushes over, perhaps attracted by hearing her name. *No*, I explain, *jasmine*. He sniffs the bouquet. *Jasmine*, he repeats, *not lavender. Jasmine.* Then he unfastens his cabbage, urging it on: *Run, Jasmine, run, run*, and he hands me the nosegay.

Last night the girls begged and begged me to go with them to the club. I like to dance, but I can't take too much of the club: the line to get in, the crowds. I ended up going anyway. I refused to dance; I just stood at the bar drinking something, and then I thought I saw my Chinese Boy, so I tried to make my way across the dance floor to find him, but he slipped away from me among the throng.

The ritual repeats itself, maybe because we tend to repeat those things we like, the ones that do us good. I'm sitting, Chinese Boy is sitting, he smiles, I smile, he says *hi*, I say *hi*, he unleashes the cabbage, I unleash Lavender. As they play (I say "they play" and I'm suddenly taken aback by that plural form), he shows me photos of a family that I understand lives very far away: two brothers and a sister, all younger, mother, father, four grandparents. They all look alike, maybe because they're Chinese. I wonder if the same thing happens to the Chinese when they see a photo of Argentines, if we all look the same to them. I also wonder if Chinese Boy isn't desperately alone.

Gastón insists that we get together, go out, talk again. I have absolutely no interest, but he persists, persists, persists till I give in. He asks me what I want to eat; I say sushi, he suggests a place, we meet there. The waiter comes over, we order. *Forks or chopsticks?* he asks us. *Forks for both of us*, Gastón says. *No, I hurriedly correct him, chopsticks for me.* The waiter walks away. Gastón regards me, perplexed. I shrug and don't tell him that one day at the park, Chinese Boy taught me how to use them, artfully manipulating the two little branches and explaining to me that in ancient times, at the Chinese imperial palace, they used silver chopsticks to determine if there was poison in the royal meals. As we eat, Gastón talks, talks, talks; I bring the Chinese chopsticks to my mouth and see Chinese Boy naked and stretched across my wide bed with violet-colored sheets that smell like violets. Every so often I reply, make a comment, and then Gastón takes up his monologue again and leaves me alone, while Chinese Boy performs a special shadow puppet show against the wall, with a fierce wolf that turns into a lamb, a rabbit that runs and stands on its hind legs to contemplate the moon, two lovers kissing.

Today Lavender is wearing barrettes with lavender bows and she looks lovely. She's jumped on and off the bench so many times that you can tell she's anxious, as if she's waiting for Chinese Boy to play with his pet again. I glance at my watch: just a while longer and I'll go, I tell myself. Then I think I hear shouts, and a few feet away from here I see Chinese Boy with his cabbage-on-a-leash, surrounded by adolescents in private high school uniforms who shout at him: *Chinese fag*, they bellow, laughing. *Does it have a pedigree?* taunts a girl with long blonde hair. *Careful, it bites!* another guy warns an older woman who steps off the sidewalk to avoid the commotion. *Does it know karate?* inquires yet another, assuming a karate expert pose and attempting a Chinese accent. *Go to your doghouse!* shouts someone else, kicking the cabbage, which, still connected to the leash, leaps into the air and falls back down onto the sidewalk. Chinese Boy doesn't do anything: he doesn't answer back, he doesn't get angry, he doesn't move, as if he were impervious or immune or absent. Seeing his lack of reaction, the kids get bored and go away. Chinese Boy remains there motionless, frozen. Lavender climbs onto my legs, taking me by surprise. I pet her; she sits and grows calm. Then I turn my head and see that Chinese Boy, fixed to the same spot, is looking in my direction. He raises one hand in the air as if to say everything's all right; he waves, which I interpret as a goodbye; he turns on his heels, picks up the cabbage, sticks it under his arm, and leaves.

Tonight there's a dinner at Franca's place; she's just returned from Germany. Irene comes to pick me up and insists I bring Lavender along. I say no, they always make her nervous, I'd rather leave her in my apartment. We get there, I greet everyone, there are just a few of us, some of whom I see often, and others I haven't seen in a while. Around one of the little living room tables, four strangers are playing Chinese checkers. Following a round of drinks, they serve sausages with sauerkraut. I play dumb, eat German bread and drink beer. I can't swallow a bite; I can't help thinking of Lavender and Jasmine on the platters, prepared and delivered by a chain of Chinese take-outs. An hour later, I'm back home with incurable nausea and an unbearable headache.

Sunday, family lunch at mom's house with some aunts and uncles who are visiting from Córdoba. I walk there, some fifteen blocks; I have time, and it's a beautiful day. Along the way I buy mascarpone ice cream, my favorite flavor, chocolate for my uncle, raspberry for mom and my aunt. First we eat eggplant à la Napolitana, then spaghetti Bolognese. *A very Mediterranean menu*, my aunt says. *Well*, I say, *almost everything, because really, I don't know if you're aware that noodles originally came from China, and the first historical reference to noodle dishes that we have were written during the Han Dynasty.* Gulp! They stare at me without daring to say a word, till mom asks me to pass the bread basket.

I'm sitting here with Lavender again, like yesterday, like the day before. But today, just when I've brought along a nosegay of lavender so that he'll finally understand what it's like, it seems Chinese Boy isn't coming. Lavender runs after a pit bull; I'm terrified, but she begs me and begs me till I think she's going to scratch my legs through my stockings, so I set her loose, and there she goes, pursuing the fearsome dog, who looks at her patiently, or compassionately, or lewdly. With my gaze lost among the trees in the background, I imagine Chinese Boy living behind the chipboard panels of some supermarket, sleeping on a mattress on the floor together with Chinese aunts, uncles, and cousins. *No understand, no understand*, says the Chinese owner of the supermarket around the corner from my building, where I sometimes buy cleaning products because Ivana told me that they're cheaper there. When someone complains to the Chinese supermarket owner about something—spoiled milk, out-of-date cold cuts, moldy cheese, he spits the refrain *No understand, no understand* in their face, while the cashier, young and also Chinese, smiles uncomfortably and fixes her slanted eyes on the merchandise, on the bills, on the floor.

I buy two Foo dog statues, replicas of the guard dogs at Buddha's temple; I place one at each side of the front door. The male—who has a ball beneath his left paw—to the left of the door; the female—who has the ball beneath her right paw—to the right, to protect me from bad energy and bad people. Lavender growls at them a couple of times but finally accepts them. Just today, after three days of downpour, it's stopped raining. In a while I'm going to take Lavender to the park, and while I'm at it, I'll break in the sneakers mom gave me for my birthday. They're a German brand, but they're made in China.

Chinese Boy hasn't returned to the park. I scour the Internet for news about the mafia. Sometimes I imagine they put him on a horrible boat and sent him back to his country. Or that they punished him for running off to the park during work hours. Every once in a while I stop by the greengrocer's and buy a cabbage for Lavender to play with. There are days when I'm sure I'm going to run into him at any moment, in the most unexpected place. Yesterday, at a second-hand bookstore, I bought a book written entirely in Chinese.

RARA AVIS

NOW, SITTING IN an evangelical church that he found open by
accident in the middle of the night, he speculates that his life
changed forever, perhaps by divine design, perhaps by a whim
of fate, that day when, on his way home from the university,
he crossed the park, backpack slung over his shoulder, taking
a shortcut to get there faster. Suddenly the facts congeal at a
point in his memory, which today, when he tries to retrieve
them, makes them appear as a single event: hearing the *plop*
of something falling straight down before his eyes; stopping in
his tracks; looking down to discover, where the rounded tips of
his sneakers ended, a thing sparsely covered by fine, brownish-
gray feathers; lifting his eyes instinctively to find the place it
came from and spotting a low-flying *chimango*; hearing the

screech of the *chimango* and at the same time watching it ascend and circle over his own head; understanding that the thing at his feet was the *chimango's* victim, and not knowing what to do till it opens one eye, and then seeing, for the first time, as if he himself had opened his eyes at that moment, the pinkness of a wound; redirecting his gaze upward and gesturing theatrically with his arms to drive the *chimango* away; seeing the *chimango* give up and leave; and then standing there alone before that thing, wounded and with one eye open, making him feel all the loneliness in the world; looking around because he doesn't know what else to do; squatting to witness how, from the mass of its upwardly-stretched body, a head and a beak emerge, and two eyes that seem to brim over with terror; extending a hand to touch; feeling the warmth and trembling, the horrific confirmation that this thing is, indeed, alive, and that he ought to do something about it. Looking all around once more, not a soul anywhere, and it's growing dark; deciding, at last, to pick up the animal, which, on being grasped from the back, extends a pair of very long legs; accommodating the creature in his left hand; feeling it curl up till it assumes the perfect shape of an egg; and walking, walking with that warm, throbbing thing, all the way home.

Putting it in a box and beginning to think about what to do, how. Not knowing where to seek help, nor what sort of creature the thing is, which, on closer examination, seems to be a pigeon chick, gangly and rustic. Surfing the Internet and coming across a couple of videos that explain everything, or nearly everything. Realizing that he urgently needs to go out again, to the pharmacy seven blocks away, to buy baby cereal, a syringe to feed it, and iodine solution to clean the wound. Once more braving the cold—more intense now because it's almost nighttime, walking, wondering why this thing had to fall from the sky, walking, arriving at the pharmacy, asking for the baby cereal and seeing how the clerk smiles at him the way you smile at a father who's good to his son and who goes shopping for his wife, but he has no son, no wife, no girlfriend, no family, nothing but that creature; wondering why he hadn't just left it where it fell so that the *chimango* might carry it off again; then asking for the syringe, and the iodine solution after that; and explaining, as if making excuses for himself, that it's to feed and heal God-knows-what kind of a chick that he found in the park; the clerk looking at him indulgently, the way you look at an idiot who's trying to revive some dumb bird; noticing that the clerk is pretty cute, but at that moment unable to summon any feeling but hatred toward her; forcing a goodbye, paying with the last of his money for the month; walking; and wondering what he'll find when he gets home; weighing the possibility that he might find it dead; inexplicably hoping he won't; picking up his pace; opening the front door; reaching the kitchen in two steps; peeking into the box and seeing it there; still vibrating, like the tuning fork he uses to tune his guitar. He goes back on the Internet, turns on the video and follows the instructions: first the iodine solution and a speck of cotton that he dips in it and gently swabs on the wound, wondering if it burns, and if in any case that burning isn't life itself. Finally he prepares the food, places it in the syringe, opens the bird's beak, introduces the paste little by little so that it won't choke, taking care not to cover its nostrils, the creature's round eyes as wide open as can be. And then a sleepless night, sleeping just a little; rising at dawn, running to check on it, watching it stand and secretly, internally, celebrating; going to the University so as not to give up the vices of the chronic student; returning home, eating something, drinking water because there's no more juice or wine; feeding the creature, and giving it water, too; having a *mate*, then a sandwich for dinner, sleeping, getting up, going to check on it, feed it, rejoicing at its hunger and how its wound is healing, going to the University, getting home, eating—both he and the creature—playing the guitar, the creature spying over the edge of the box, then sleeping, getting up, going to check, taking it out of the box, watching it suddenly move, eat, shit, drink water, growing unbelievably fast, and suddenly thinking that what fell out of the sky is something like a *ñandú*, and one day shooing it out to the little square of grass on his tiny patio, drinking, eating, sleeping, shitting—he and the ever-expanding creature that looks more and more like a *ñandú*; noticing one day (but he's already losing sight of which day it is) that a strange, hard thing is growing on its head, and one afternoon seeing some black feathers pop out, silky and fine as hairs, and noting that the protuberance on its head is turning into something like a bony crest, and beginning to imagine that it's not a *ñandú*, that it has to be something else; and consulting with a veterinary student who says no, no idea, but he'll try to find out; and getting up in the middle of the night, after a murky nightmare, and going over to the counter for a glass of water, looking out at the little patio, determining that the creature's face and part of its neck are completely covered with minuscule rainbow-colored feathers, and standing there, staring, the creature, in turn, with its now enormous feet, staring right back at him. Becoming aware that by now it must come up to his knees, and realizing, after surfing the Internet, that what he has in his house is a cassowary, an Australian bird, huge and solitary, flightless and potentially very aggressive, with its sharp talons and rigid crest, even to the point of causing human deaths. Wondering again and again where that Australian cassowary might have come from, thrown to his feet by a *chimango*, in any case a local species; wondering, incidentally, why him, and beginning to doubt everything, the *chimango*, the entire episode, his memory, his eyes, which now contemplate the oversize creature, strange and lovely, curled up in one corner of the patio. And unable to feel fear or fright, but only sorrow for it, a cold, blue sorrow; deciding then to find a more appropriate home for it, asking here and there, taking it to a neighbor's farm, but it doesn't last long there, having kicked against the wire fence with its talons and frightened the dogs, the chickens. Discovering, when they return it to him, that the creature recognizes him, producing very strange, but friendly, sounds—as if communicating with one of its own—and lies down at his feet. Receiving offers, then, from people who want to buy it, fearing the intentions of some of those people, finding out that there's a *vedette* in Buenos Aires who wants to make herself an outfit from the exotic plumage of his cassowary, seeing it plucked alive, to prevent its plumes from losing their shine and to allow for the possibility of their growing back; becoming aware, also, of clandestine animal fights, fights to the death, on the outskirts of the city, and feeling nausea and disgust at the mere idea of having saved the creature just to hand it over to its death or to a hellish life in exchange for a few pesos; trying to get in touch with environmental associations to return the cassowary to its habitat, but finding it too expensive and impractical; allowing it to enter the apartment, so as not to confine it to the territorial meagerness of his patio; knowing that this decision is like resigning himself to chaos and the unforeseen; sharing spaces, being invaded, becoming even more disorganized than he was before; looking it in the eye one day and realizing that things can't go on like this and once again not knowing what to do. Finding himself one afternoon in the midst of his turmoil, peeling an orange and hearing a gut-wrenching screech coming from the patio and going outside just like that: startled, with a half-peeled orange in one hand and a knife in the other; seeing it come toward him, and suddenly, without knowing how, understanding that the knife blade has disappeared and lodged itself in the dense black plumage beneath its maw; detecting a bit of blood spurting out; suddenly managing to kneel and receive the cassowary's head, which falls, like an offering, against his chest, the serene eyes fixed on him, and all the turquoise of the head and neck feathers spilling over his hands.

When he looks backward, that is what he can see: a living thing, which turned out to be a cassowary, falling on him from the sky, and he, no longer knowing where to go, now sitting in that church, hearing a talk about the end of the world, his hands tinted a blazing, iridescent turquoise that he hasn't been able to remove, no matter how hard he's tried.

NEKO CAFÉ

SUDDENLY I STOP, my bicycle between my legs, my feet resting on the sidewalk, in order to look through the window of the Neko Café. A blonde server waits on a couple sitting beside a cat on one of the long sofas in the place. The boy, his body tilted slightly forward, pronounces a phrase that I can't quite hear because of the distance, the thick glass that stands between them and me, and also because of the incessant noise of cars in the street, but no doubt he's ordering coffee for both of them and something for the cat. The girlfriend leans against the back of the sofa and caresses the enormous animal, fascinated: she runs her fingers through its soft fur, both of them with eyes half-closed; you can tell that both the animal and the woman are enjoying it. The cat is a Ragdoll, characterized by its extremely docile character. I've always been a big fan of cats, curious about the various breeds, which I've read about, and still do, all the time.

When the server turns toward the counter to relay the orders, I can see her better, her long, long, slender white legs, the very short, naturally blonde hair with bangs swept to one side and one delicate lock tinted green. She's not Japanese, nor is she some casual tourist, most likely a traveler who has decided to stick around here for a while. Following her, with its tail raised high and probably meowing, is what I take to be a Havana Brown, an exquisite cat, slender and dark, hard to find except in photos; actually I can't get over my astonishment at having it just a few meters away from me. I've never been able to have a cat; to have a cat in Tokyo you practically need to be rich; there's no space in this city, rental units are tiny and hard to keep up, which is why people come to places like this or else buy stuffed animals in the form of cats and become obsessed with recognizing cat breeds. There's not much time, either: people spend most of the day rushing from one place to another, working, eating, bathing, sleeping; it's costly to live here, and exhausting.

A young boy who looks like a sumo wrestler, very fat and with a ponytail, kneels and crawls to get closer to a white Japanese Bobtail with black ears, one of those domestic cats with a short tail like a bunny, orange with brown spots. The sumo wrestler extends his hand, the cat looks at him and allows itself to be petted, then comes close and sits at his side. To the left, a young man walks in wearing torn jeans, the kind that have been ripped on purpose, and a white business shirt like mine; he has on dark glasses and a surgical mask; most likely he's got the flu, or maybe he's one of those people who are afraid of germs; he's wearing the classic gray slippers they offer you when you come in, if you don't want to go around in stocking feet. It's not that I know this from personal experience, because I've never been inside a neko café, but I have an office mate who sometimes goes to these places, and apparently they're all similar: when you walk in there's a hall with cubbies, where you leave your shoes, and there's a piece of furniture with slippers that are part of the service if you want to put them on; then you need to wash your hands with antiseptic gel in order not to bring bacteria or germs into the place; then you get a card that shows the time you arrived, because you pay by the hour, in addition to paying for whatever you consume; and finally you reach a place that's like a café, where the cats are, too.

I'm startled by a light tap against my leg; another cyclist has entered the scene; I look at him, annoyed; bicycles swarm around here and there, and pedestrians too; he shrugs and continues on his way. Two more cats, a Manx and a mixed-breed, have climbed up on the sofa where the couple is and watch the Ragdoll eat from a feeding bowl, delicately, what I imagine to be chicken or fish, while the couple drinks their coffee. Now I see that it's definitely chicken; from the way the Ragdoll chews and swallows, you can infer its texture, more compact than fish, which easily falls apart in the mouth. The truth is that I'm very good at deducing, imagining, hypothesizing; I should have continued my education instead of being a simple office worker, chosen a career where confirming theories and keeping one step ahead of the facts can prove useful.

The blonde server, in her loose white tee shirt, short black skirt, white anklets, and red slippers, waits on other customers who are away from the window, more toward the inside of the place. A very tall, red-haired man has just arrived and takes a seat on a large cushion on the carpet, next to the library. The young man in the dark glasses and surgical mask also walks toward the library to choose a book; from what I've been told, all the books in these places have to do with cats, I don't know how he's supposed to read in those glasses he never takes off. The redhead pulls out a cell phone, another server comes over swiftly and explains something to him, the man nods, presses a button, then takes a picture, without a flash, of a Serengeti that's poised before him like a miniature leopard, its face raised, its tail hanging. You're not allowed to use a flash in these places, so that the animals won't get frightened or nervous. My office mate didn't tell me that; I know because I read it in a magazine in a waiting room. The Ragdoll has finished eating and is stretched out next to the young woman of the couple, who's now rubbing its belly. Ragdolls adore their owners and don't like to be alone.

A Persian cat jumps down from an individual perch on one of the side walls and looks like it's about to come my way. The redhead gets up and walks over to another cat, with tiger-like fur, who's asleep on a perch, with the idea of taking a photo, I suppose. It seems he prefers cats with fur like the larger felines. You're not allowed to wake or disturb sleeping animals; my office mate didn't tell me that, either, we don't talk all that much. I read it recently on the Internet. The Persian comes over to the window and stays there, watching me; it's not one of my favorite breeds, maybe because I prefer stylized cats with long legs and short hair, like the Devon Rex, but I haven't seen one of those here, or the exotic Havana Brown, which for a while now has been following the blonde server around. Now she leans over toward him, strokes his head; he arches his back and lifts his tail; she places a little bowl of milk on a low table for him; the Havana leaps on the table, brings his nose over to the milk but doesn't drink. A couple of cats have gathered around the table, eager, no doubt, for that milk, though it doesn't look as though they'll dare fight him over it. The Havana Brown has a bearing and an expression that impose respect. Meanwhile, the Persian cat has arrived at the window and plants itself next to a sign that says: "1000 yen or 10 dollars an hour." Just now it lifts its paw in the air as though beckoning me to come in; it looks like a copy of the gold *maneki-neko* that stands on a display table against the window, to the right of the sign, inviting customers inside. Seeing that it's gotten no response, the Persian turns around indifferently, returns to the center of the place and walks over to a system of tubes that rise to the ceiling, covered in layers and layers of sisal, to which a series of cushion-lined baskets are connected. It leaps up, reaches the first basket, scratches the rough fabric covering the section of tubing within reach of its claws, gathers momentum, takes another leap and rises to the second basket, sniffs it, jumps onto the cushion that covers it and stretches out. The Havana Brown has climbed down from the little table and walks away; then the cats who were anxiously waiting both scramble up and start to drink from the bowl. The Havana Brown jumps on the counter and there he sits; from here I can admire his perfect, effigy-like profile.

Two girls dressed in high-school uniforms, blue blazer with a shield, white shirt, little blue-and-white kerchief around their necks, and short, pleated skirts, are having fun in an area to my left, playing with a gray British Shorthair that resembles a stuffed animal with huge, fat cheeks and round, intensely yellow eyes. One of the girls dangles a cord with tassels and colored ribbons at the end. The cat flips onto its back on the carpet and lifts its front paws to catch the tassels and ribbons. The other girl watches them, laughing, apparently finding it very amusing. The boy with the dark glasses and surgical mask has taken a seat at one of the rear tables with a book he selected from the library. From here I can see that he's wearing thin latex gloves, the kind nurses or doctors use. I don't know when he could have put them on, no doubt at some point when my attention was elsewhere. He opens the book at random and, instead of reading, starts observing the other people around him. He's the strangest of all the characters in the place. I have the idea he's one of those hypochondriacs who are always on alert, discovering threats to their health everywhere. I find his presence disturbing and at the same time contradictory: if you're afraid of catching something, the logical decision would be not to go to a relatively small place crowded with people and cats.

Two smartly dressed middle-aged women walk in, cross the room in front of the masked boy, and sit down at a table quite close to the window, and by extension, to me. Then I lower my eyes for a moment so as not to attract attention, pretending I'm going to reorganize the things I'm carrying in my bicycle basket. The blonde server comes over to take their order; she has green eyes and a minuscule piercing, which I hadn't noticed before, in her nose. She's very pretty and chats pleasantly with the women, in Japanese I deduce, judging from the movement of her lips. How strange, I say to myself, and I like her even more. Suddenly the Havana Brown gets up, leaps off the counter, walks straight ahead, crosses paths with the blonde server, who's heading toward the counter to

turn in the newly-arrived customers' orders. With the airiest
of leaps, he lands on the women's table, and sits on something
like a round plastic placemat bearing the black silhouette of
a cat in the center, also seated, like the Havana's shadow. The
women, one with a round face, the other with a slender one,
regard him with joy and astonishment and there the animal
remains, calm and erect as a king, or rather a god, ready to
receive all the praise they may want to lavish, and in fact
are lavishing, on him, with smiles and gentle movements of
carefully manicured, beringed hands. Behind the tableau of
the women, the red-haired man walks up to the counter on the
left, a few meters from the collection of cat books, shows the
blonde server the card indicating his time of arrival, takes out
his wallet, and pays. The ponytailed sumo wrestler reclines
on the carpet, his head resting on the cushion he had been
sitting on earlier. The Japanese Bobtail he was petting a few
minutes ago and a mixed-breed cat, which I hadn't noticed
before because it was probably asleep in a corner, come up to
him, climb on top of his body, and are now walking on him;
they march up and down their improvised, padded catwalk,
moving their tails sensuously. He laughs and strokes them.
The boy in dark glasses, mask, and latex gloves is still sitting
at his table in the back, with the open book in his hands; there
are no cats around him, and I repeat something I've always
told myself: I don't trust people who animals reject or avoid.
The couple that was sitting on the sofa with the Ragdoll gets
up and walks toward the counter, crossing paths with the
redhead, who is heading to the right of me, most likely to the
entry hall, to leave his slippers and put on his street shoes.
Maybe it's almost closing time; I should go, too, and yet I
stay here watching the blonde server approach the women's

table again, this time bringing a tray with two shakes that she drops off in front of them, and a blue ceramic bowl that she deposits on the placemat beside the Havana Brown, who, stubbornly maintaining his idol pose, doesn't budge. One of the women, the one with the plump face, pushes the bowl up to the cat's nose; he sniffs the contents but doesn't eat, as if he were beyond the needs of any living being. The woman puts the bowl down, exchanges a look with her companion, they both smile, raise their glasses in unison and take a sip of their foamy, white shakes.

The high school students are surrounded by three cats— the Manx and the Ragdoll have joined the British Shorthair they were playing with and who haven't stopped jumping on and off the sofa where they're hanging out, stimulated by the ribbons and toys the girls are using to prod them. When a Ragdoll is picked up it has a tendency to loosen its muscles and relax completely, becoming soft and inert like a rag doll, but that can't be demonstrated here because they don't let people pick up the cats in their arms. This was once explained to me by a supplier who comes to the office and frequents these places; it's one of the rules of neko cafés.

The other server goes over to the guy in glasses, mask, and gloves, to take his order, I guess, though I can't be sure; he refuses whatever she asked him by shaking his head and lowering his gaze toward the book he's still holding, open to the same page as when he first picked it up, I'll bet. The server walks away from his table and approaches the beefy wrestler, who, seeing her from the floor, quickly rises, sits, smiles at her; the cats climb onto his lap and he orders something. The server continues on her way to the counter.

Again I focus my attention on the young man in the surgical mask; then he lifts his head and looks in this direction, as if he knows I'm watching him or as if he can read my mind and understand what I'm thinking about him, though to tell the truth, those dark glasses of his prevent me from knowing if he's fixing his gaze on the women who are finishing their shakes, on the glass window, the now-illuminated street lamps, the vaguely Egyptian profile of the Havana Brown, the *maneki-neko*, which he's probably seeing from the back, or on me. He closes the book, stands, takes a few steps; I think he's going to come over here to intimidate me or call attention to me, or maybe he's signaling to one of the servers that I'm out here, looking in. Instead, though, he walks over to the library and carefully replaces the book on one of the shelves. Unexpectedly, the Ragdoll, who a few moments ago was playing with the students, is now walking around over there and approaches him; the boy looks at him, barely touches him with the tip of his toe, and just as I'm beginning to doubt my previous suspicions, once more turns his head in my direction: his appearance is so unusual and he acts so strange that I briefly imagine at any moment he might pull out a weapon and kill any animal or human that crosses his path. And everything would become a desperate, human-animal cry that would be extinguished, swallowed by the street noise and its indifferent din, and me, stuck here to this spot, unable to move or to do anything. They would all fall, one after another, like in a Shakespearean tragedy: the sumo wrestler with the ponytail, laid out on the carpet, surrounded by his now motionless cats; the other server with her torso splayed across the counter; the couple a few steps from the front door; the fallen students, one on top of the other, their floppy arms suddenly releasing the little toys with which they so joyfully amused the cats and themselves; the ring-bedecked women, their heads drooping forward beside the overturned, broken milkshake glasses; animals scattered like stains on the dark carpet; the blonde girl, liquid and spilled upon a table, her long, slender white legs, now flaccid as rags. And then will come the abandonment of the print-free weapon on the counter, the dash to the entry hall, the retrieval of sneakers and the quick escape, slippers held in gloved hands and feet wrapped in socks to avoid wasting time or leaving footprints. In the commotion, the door to the place will of necessity be left open so that the Havana Brown, slightly stunned, can escape, and before choosing his route he will stop for a moment on the opaque sidewalk, less trafficked at this time of day, right in front of me, so that at last I can study him, without glass between us, dark and beautiful as the shadow of a cruel god.

AS IF THE WORLD WERE ENDING

ENNIO'S ARRIVAL WAS a miracle, as if someone or something had told him that we needed him in this house. The day before, Señor Esteban, who for years had taken care of the garden, was attacked and beaten and ended up in the hospital, poor thing. Señora Andrea was terribly worried, because you know how she gets when spring is on its way: the plants seem to go crazy, growing and growing relentlessly and taking over everything. She used to tell anyone who was willing to listen that she had moved from the apartment to the house so that she could have plants and be in contact with nature, that it relaxed her when she came home from recording hours and hours of soap operas for TV.

I remember I was in the upstairs bedroom, changing the sheets on Señora Andrea's bed, when the intercom buzzed. I flew downstairs; the house is big, and the señora doesn't like it when people keep buzzing; it makes her nervous. A peaceful household is very important to her. I answered the door, of course, and I could see him through the peephole: he had come to offer his services as a gardener. He was nice-looking, and said, in a kind of strange accent, that he had references. I asked him to wait while I went to ask the señora.

I don't know what they talked about a little later, when the señora had finished bathing and received him, or what kind of reference papers he showed her, if, in fact, he showed her any, but she told me that Ennio would come back that same afternoon to start working on the garden. I was to let him in through the garage entrance, which was the one I used for coming and going, as did the dog walker, the seltzer man, and the supermarket delivery boy.

He slept with me, it's true, in the room where I sleep, because I've been a live-in maid here for years. Well, not really all that long in this place because Señora Andrea moved here two years ago. But I had already been working for her at the apartment. At first the señora didn't know that Ennio spent his nights here. It's just that when he told me the things that had happened to him and that he had nowhere to go, I couldn't refuse, and so I let him stay. It was so nice to listen to him, with his strange way of speaking. Besides, he told me things that were so ... and he looked at me in a way that's hard to explain, but later I found out why Ennio was the way he was, with that strength he had in his whole body and that wild sort of smell that made me think about nothing but taking him to bed with me. He would brush against me as he passed by, and

66

the rest of that day I couldn't think of anything else. I wished with all my soul that the hours would pass quickly and soon it would be time for him to go, so that Señora Andrea would see him leave, and later that night, I would secretly open the door for him so he could come in and stay. Together we ate whatever I brought up to my room, and when we were done we'd climb into bed.

Later on we stopped pretending that he was leaving, and he stayed behind in my room. Till one day Señora Andrea found out, got very angry, and called him over to have a talk with her. I don't know what explanation he gave her, because in the end Señora Andrea made me take everything out of the little room where she used to store boxes of photos, boxes of her films, and cut-out articles from old magazines and trophies and plaques for the prizes she'd won, carry the boxes up to the attic and make up a bed for him in the emptied space. He accepted the offer, but in fact he always stayed and slept with me.

At first I didn't even pay attention to what was wrong with Ennio; he made me so hot I couldn't think, he made me blind, he had a way of touching me that even now I can't think about it without wanting him here, close to me, again. It must have been about a week later that I woke up needing to pee and then I saw him and realized that he had gone to bed in his sneakers. They were sticking out from under the slightly lifted sheets. It seemed strange, of course, but I thought he had collapsed after working all day among the plants, with the shovel, the pruning shears, climbing up and down trees, lugging rocks in the wheelbarrow for some new flower beds, and, on top of it all, everything we'd done in bed. But honestly I didn't say anything to him because I didn't want him to feel uncomfortable and go away. My life had changed so much since he arrived ... Why would I want to ruin everything with my big mouth?

He had a passion for plants and trees that I've never seen in anyone else, not even a gardener. He would grab handfuls of earth and smell them like they were a bottle of perfume. He would climb trees so quickly and gracefully that he didn't seem to weigh an ounce. But he wasn't scrawny; in fact he was pretty muscular, and I liked to feel all his weight on me, his chest, his arms, run my hands over his hairy back. In bed he was like an animal.

Señora Andrea's dogs loved him, the poodle and the Afghan; sometimes they fought over who would play with him. He got them to do whatever he wanted: fetch things for him, play dead, bury bones, or fight with one another. I told him: they're going to wear themselves out; if Señora Andrea sees you, she'll be angry. They're dogs, Ennio would reply, sometimes they've got to act like dogs. And besides, Señora Andrea never gets angry with me.

He could also do anything with plants: he shaped them, he made them burst with flowers, he could take one that at first glance looked dry and dead and make it bloom again in no time at all. The same with people. He stripped away my willpower; all I wanted was to please him and for him to keep doing everything he did to me in bed, even though he never took off his sneakers, and sometimes, for that very reason, he left me with bruises or scraped legs.

After a while he started to change a little. And he would disappear in the middle of the night. I walked over to his room and opened the door carefully to see if he was asleep.

Since he was never there, I would look out the window that faces the garden and sometimes I'd see him, up in the walnut tree, staring at Señora Andrea's room, or at the moon. Other times he wasn't in his room or in the garden, and I didn't see him anywhere. I started to suspect that he had left the house. Sometimes I heard him whispering on his cell phone. He seemed a little more distant, and certain things I did began to annoy him.

On one of those nights when I looked out to see where he was, I thought I saw a shadow climbing up to the balcony outside Señora Andrea's room. But how could I be sure when we'd had some liquor, a yellow liquor, like gold, that Ennio had brought, according to him, to celebrate. To celebrate what? I asked, thinking he was going to propose something. To celebrate life, he said. And after a glass, he pulled down my panties and fucked me against the wall just like that, half-dressed. When I woke up he wasn't there. I looked out the window, and that was when I thought I saw the shadow. I waited for Señora Andrea to scream, turn on the light, or make some sign or call for help, but I heard nothing and saw nothing, so I went back to bed.

One day we had an ugly fight. That afternoon a guy with a face I didn't like at all showed up at the door. I told the guy that Ennio wasn't there, that he'd gone out; to Ennio I didn't say a word. We had been drinking a little again, and I asked him why the fuck he never took off his sneakers. Yeah, that's exactly how I said it, why the fuck, very rudely, because the fact is I felt slightly jealous. And that's when he told me the secret, he told me it was something he kept hidden and that nobody needed to know, because when people found out about it they stopped loving him, or else they wanted to take

69

control of him, of his life, and he couldn't belong to anyone. He had a problem with his feet, he said; he'd been born that way, and it wasn't really a problem for him, but for everyone else it was. And that he'd gotten used to nobody seeing his feet. Whenever his secret came out in the open, sooner or later he had to leave wherever he was. That's how his life had been, he told me. He went over to the little dresser, stuck his hand in his jacket pocket, took something out, and then he came closer and showed me a picture of a lovely fountain in Italy, in Florence. I didn't catch the name of the place, something that sounded like *plaza* and like *señora* or *señoría*. He said that he had come from there, traveling from town to town, from one country to another, looking for a place to stay, to settle down. That he was like the one in the fountain, and he pointed to a statue that looked a lot like him, a whole lot; then he went on talking in another language that I guessed was Italian because I couldn't understand a word anymore. I was going to ask him so very many things ... but he grew pale and he looked so awful that I decided to keep quiet.

Then he started to cry. And right then and there I felt rotten for doing that to him; I apologized, I kissed him, I undressed him carefully, leaving his sneakers on; I put him to bed and stayed there watching him till he fell asleep.

Another night I woke up suddenly, startled. Ennio was sleeping like a log, maybe still a little bit drunk. Then I couldn't stand it anymore; I wanted to know the secret, and I couldn't control myself any longer, so I tiptoed over to him slowly and began to untie one of his shoelaces. But it was a disaster, because he took notice, sat up quickly in bed, looked at me with a fury that came from who-knows-where, and shook his legs; I had to jump backwards so he wouldn't kick me; then he leaped out of bed, came right up to me, I was petrified, he started shoving me around and said he didn't expect that of me, me of all people. I felt awful, guilty, like a piece of garbage: he was right. He must've understood how I felt because his anger faded, he tried to calm me down, and in the end he took my hands gently, led me to the bed, asked me to sit down. He sat down too, kissed me, and said: All right, do you want to know my secret? I'll tell you, but then I'll have to go. Unfortunately, things always turn out this way.

No, I replied, forget about everything, don't tell me. I'd been a fool. It didn't matter anymore that he had a secret, or deformed feet, or whatever it was; I didn't want him to go. But he insisted that I was the one who had made it end up like this and there was no other way out. And then he confessed it to me, he confessed he was a faun. A faun? I asked, practically shouting. He covered my mouth with one hand, saying shhh. Then he explained that he had a man's body, but with hooves. Hooves? I repeated, now in a quiet voice and not really understanding him, while I couldn't help directing my eyes toward his sneakers. Like a goat's, he explained. A goat? It seemed nothing else would come out of my mouth except a repetition of what he said to me, but in the form of a question. Yes, I'm a faun; that's why I need to be in contact with nature, keep my feet—well, hooves—on the earth; that's why at night I escape to the garden, and when no one is watching I take off my sneakers and climb the tree or stand among the plants. That nourishes my life, gives me all the strength I have and need after so many years. What do you mean, so many years? I blurted, astonished. You're even younger than I am. What we see is one thing, he explained, what is, is another. To be honest, it all seemed incredible to me, but, I don't know why, I also believed him and was sure it was true. Now I could explain so many things ... Then I remembered the little goats my sisters and I used to raise in the mountains of my province. Suddenly I felt very sad; I asked him for forgiveness and begged him not to go away; I swore not to tell anyone. He didn't reply, we went to bed, we embraced, and he talked to me about fauns till we both fell asleep.

It must have been around daybreak when I thought I heard some noises I couldn't quite identify, footsteps, running, maybe, something like a door squeaking, but my sleep and my body felt so heavy that I couldn't wake up.

When I finally awoke it was late and Ennio was gone. I changed quickly, and while I was making breakfast, Señora Andrea came by to ask for him. I said I hadn't seen him. She stiffened. What do you mean, you didn't see him? You've got to know where he is! she screamed furiously, You've got to know! I didn't understand a thing, señor, not one thing, till you arrived and then I started to understand a little.

The only thing I can tell you is that Ennio is innocent. When the thieves showed up, they must've seen him sitting up in the tree, with his hooves resting on the bark of the tree, looking at the moon like he did so many times, with the dogs asleep at his feet. And then he had no choice but to run away and escape without thinking of anything or anyone, to look for a new place to live. Why didn't the dogs bark? How should I know! They aren't guard dogs. Besides, look, how can you not believe me when his sneakers are here? They were at the foot of the walnut tree. C'mon, man, use your head. Why do you think Señora Andrea wants to find him? Go on, tell me why she hired you instead of calling the police. Not because of the things the thieves took. No, that's not why, believe me. Do you want to know why? It's because Ennio went away, and if you don't find him, he'll never crawl into her bed again and pleasure her as if, at that very moment, the world was about to end.

PROCEED
WITH CAUTION

THE FIRST TIME I saw him was last summer. It was very hot, and I had left the window open; a gentle breeze barely stirred the curtains. I had turned off the lights to keep out the mosquitos; the TV was on, filling the room with a flickering blue glow. Then I had the sensation that something had slipped from the window into my room. At first I imagined a cat, but the bulk I perceived was too big. For a while, I waited expectantly. Then I thought I had imagined it and continued to watch an old, black-and-white film they were showing on the government channel, and I ended up falling asleep. In the middle of the night, as often happens, I had to get up to go to the bathroom. The TV was still on. As I placed my feet on the floor in search of my slippers, I saw him: it was an enormous dog with a dark head and short, dense fur. I put on my glasses, which I kept on the nightstand, and leaned over a little to see him better. He was asleep, curled up in a ball. I kept still, waiting for him to wake up or move, but there was absolutely no reaction. I've always liked dogs, but I also know that when you aren't familiar with an animal, it's best to be cautious. So I dismissed the idea of putting on my slippers, stealthily got up from the other side of the bed, and walked barefoot to the bathroom. When I returned, the dog was sitting on his hind legs, looking at me. *What's this lovely boy doing here in my room?* I said, as I turned off the TV set. He smiled at me the way dogs smile, not with his mouth, but with his eyes. I moved closer to him, briefly stroked his head, which came up to my waist, and went back to bed. I heard him lie down on the floor again, and I went back to sleep. In the morning he was no longer there. I had the impression I had dreamed it.

He has a dog's face, but he looks nothing like Rocky. My daughter gave Rocky to me when Ernesto died. So many years married to Ernesto … and it's not that I was still in love with him, but we were very good companions, and living with him was peaceful. When he passed away, I felt like an orphan, like an amputee, and then Graciela showed up with Rocky in a little basket. *It's a stuffed animal*, I said. *No, Mom, it's a golden retriever*, she replied. And yes, he was a golden retriever; that's why he liked to chase things, so I would toss him a sock, a slipper, a ball, anything, and he would take off running and bring it back to me right away. What a fine dog; I had him with me for fourteen years.

Were you out partying last night? Amanda asked as soon as she saw me. *Or have you started putting on lipstick before you go to bed? My lips were chapped*, I replied, *and I have no cocoa butter.* But she knows I'm lying to her, and I, in turn, know what she's thinking and doesn't dare say: I'm such a flirt that if death comes for me at night, I'd want to be found the next day with my lipstick on. I laugh to myself. No, what she's thinking doesn't even come close to the truth, absolutely not. *You did the right thing*, she clarifies. *Chapped lips are very annoying. You always understand me, Amanda*, I respond.

Last night we ate the candies that I asked Amanda to buy for me. They came in an exquisite little box and contained an assortment of chocolates filled with different nuts and liqueurs. We also watched *Tabú*, a Portuguese film, in which, practically from the very first scene, an explorer on an expedition—depressed by the death of his young wife, whom he adored—disappears into a swamp and allows himself to be devoured by a crocodile. He was fascinated by this scene and didn't take his eyes off the screen, except to gulp down another candy. I ate two or three, and he polished off the rest. No doubt about it: he's ravenous.

One afternoon there was a meeting on the patio of the residence. It was a lovely day, and they had given permission to invite that girl who reads cards and entertains the women so much. I'm not a fan of that sort of thing: I don't believe in anything, and in fact it bores me. But that day I was sad, because no one from my family had come to visit me during the week. I understand that there are so few of us: I'm a widow and I have no sisters; my cousin Agustina lives very far away and is worse off than me; my daughter and granddaughter work a lot and are always busy. But their visits, talking with them, does me good. And the truth is that they come very seldom and are always in a hurry. But I understand them anyway: when you're young, there's never enough time; when you're old, time goes by slowly, it stretches out like an infinite jest. Well, the thing is, that day I went out to the garden and walked over to the table. The girl was reading Dora's cards. I stood there watching, and then, suddenly, I discovered it—one of the cards had his picture on it. I adjusted my eyeglasses and moved my chair a little closer to the table. He wasn't naked, of course; he was wearing something like a little skirt, and on top another garment that covered his chest, and a kind of necklace, but not with beads like the ones we women wear, but rather metal all over, with a design of kings or Egyptian gods or something, and some embossed bracelets. But what impressed me the most was that his body was just the same: skinny, kind of a broad back, but not too broad, and the head of a black dog. When the girl had finished, I asked her if I could take a closer look at the card. She explained what it meant and also what it was called: a name I forgot right away, and another one that's like what I call him now, because—since he doesn't talk—he never told me his name, and I've got to call him something.

I explain that he's got to be careful with the security cameras at the residence. He just stares at me without even blinking. Then I go to the shelf and pick up the map I requested from the guard and left there, folded up. I told the guard that it made me feel safer to know where the cameras were located. I walk over to the table and pull out a chair. And I also told the guard that my daughter wanted to see a map or something with that information. The guard replied that he had to consult the administration, but early the next day, there he was, knocking on my door with a copy of the map in his hand. I sit down. My daughter's the one who pays, so they couldn't refuse her alleged request. I summon him over and he stops beside me, lays his dark snout on the table, observes the map attentively. Then, suddenly, he opens that big maw of his and, before I can react or stick out my hand to retrieve the piece of paper, he's already grabbed it between his teeth, chewed it savagely, and swallowed it. *I think I'm going to have to teach you good manners*, I say. He lowers his ears and gazes at me with the most bewitching eyes in the world.

At this age, getting up and walking is no easy task. My body hurts. And it's that pain, added to all the abilities that you start losing—becoming slower and clumsier—that gives the body an inescapable, sometimes unbearable, presence. When I was young, I used my body, though it was barely a body: I felt so healthy and light that I hardly ever thought about it. Now, on the other hand, in my old age, I am always a body, a body that hurts, a body that doesn't respond, a body that my head always has to carry around on its back. A body that weighs tons, even though I'm as skinny as a wire.

One day—out of pure habit that remained from my time with Rocky—I had the idea to throw him a slipper, to see what he would do. First he followed its trajectory with his eyes without moving from his spot. But no sooner had the slipper hit the ground than he leaped toward it, picked it up between his teeth, shook it a couple of times, and suddenly gulped it down. I stood there, dumbstruck. I must confess I didn't know whether to laugh or to start fearing him. It was then that I understood that he could eat anything. And that each time he came he was going to eat something, something that wasn't dog food, but rather sustenance for a monster or a capricious god.

No, not the TV, I tell him, *because then I'll be bored.* It's not that I watch so often or pay too much attention to it, but I leave it on in the background for company. With the voices, of course, but also with that flickering blue glow that's projected against the walls. He looks at me, not saying a word, but I know he understands me. He's going to eat something else instead, that's for sure. But I'm not complaining—what can I say? Life is a transaction, and we all know it.

I read less and less all the time. It gives me a headache; it's hard for me to concentrate. Maybe I need to change my eyeglass prescription, but I'm exhausted by the mere prospect of having to go to the ophthalmologist, being examined, then getting the prescription, visiting the optician a couple of times, all of it depending on the availability of someone to go along with me both ways, considering how terribly slow and wobbly I am. I've always been a reader: reading was a refuge for me, but now I don't know—I open a book, I start out eagerly, and soon I get bored, as if I can't find anything interesting anymore. Maybe I'll tell the cynocephalus to eat some books; if he leaves me just a couple, that should be more than enough.

Every time he leaves, I have to shake out the quilt a little. He's developed the habit of curling up in a ball on the bed when I fall asleep, and I know for a fact that he sleeps there. I can't catch him in the act, because he's very clever and makes me believe, among other things, that he likes to lounge on the sofa. And yet sometimes, even though I'm half asleep, I turn around and feel his warmth nearby. On other occasions, I've stretched my legs and touched his loin or his back—I never know how to refer to him and his parts, like a person or like a dog. The thing is, when I wake up, he's almost always gone. And there's a hollow left in the bed. *He's really not all that clever after all.* I smile as I shake the quilt to get rid of the hairs he's left on top of it, before Amanda shows up to clean.

The first time he stood before me on two feet, I was so shocked that it left me speechless. In that posture he didn't look so much like a dog, but rather like a person. On the inside, or what until that moment had been underneath, he was almost as hairless as a human being. I was used to my golden retriever, who was so hairy, inside and out, or on top and underneath, according to the angle from which you looked at him. Well, the thing is, the cynocephalus was not; he had no hair on his chest, or on his groin, or anywhere else ... So he looked too naked. *You can't go through life like that, showing everything,* I said to him. This time I realized he hadn't understood me. Then I pointed out his parts to him. I must say, it had been many years since I saw such a large, youthful member. I explained that he had to get dressed, to wear clothes. Then, suddenly, it was clear that he had understood something, because he returned to his position on all fours. That way, with his hair (sparse as it was) covering his back and part of his limbs, he didn't seem quite so bare. I walked over to the closet and took out a bathrobe. I pointed it out to him, showed him how to put it on, left it on the sofa. As soon as I turned my back on him to return to bed, he leaped over to the sofa and put it on; I don't know if I've mentioned how tremendously agile he was. When I finished tucking myself in, he was standing upright again, but with the bathrobe on. And I must admit that it left quite an impression on me, because he looked very, very much like the figure on the Tarot card that I'd seen the girl in the garden holding that afternoon. I was also astonished by how beautiful he was.

Today I asked my granddaughter to bring me a set of boy's clothes. *A shirt like Gastón's*, I explained, *with a checkered pattern ... and preferably blue.* I didn't tell her that blue would look good on the cynocephalus, but I thought it would. *And underwear. And a pair of jeans, the worn-out kind they wear nowadays.* She gave me a strange look, so I invented the story that I had seen the gardener so poorly dressed that I felt sorry for him. She offered to bring me some of the clothing her boyfriend no longer used. I said yes, so that she wouldn't suspect me, but asked her to please add that new set of clothing I had requested. *I don't like to give away only discards; that's not real charity*, I suddenly blurted out. *You're so sweet, Gran*, she replied with a smile.

Early this morning, before he left and while I was sleeping, he devoured a chunk of wall opposite my bed, leaving a dark spot there that frightens me a little. As I don't want to be paralyzed with fear like that, I decide to take a closer look. First I extend my cane, lest I fall forward into that hole. But the darkness produces no sound, even though I tap it a little with the tip of the cane. Then I approach, bend forward and downward, preparing to feel something unpleasant, and I rest my hand. But I don't feel anything—pleasant or unpleasant, hot or cold, rough or smooth. And I imagine that the blackness before me must be the nothingness that he exposes with each bite. Today I'm going to tell him to help me move the sofa, so no one will see that threatening thing.

The other night he showed up with the clothes I had given him, a little stained, and when he came close to my bed I smelled beer. However, he behaved the same as always: he sat down beside me, put his hand on top of mine, and listened to the news of the day. I talk to him more than to anyone else. He listens to me, gestures, and, depending on what I tell him, he changes the expression in his eyes, which gives me the idea that, in his way, he understands me. Finally, he fell asleep while I was talking to him, and I didn't have the nerve to throw him out of bed, so I covered him with the quilt, and that's where I left him.

Not long ago he ate the shelf where my family portraits were: the photo of my wedding to Abelardo; the one of Arielito's First Communion; his military service portrait; the one of Graciela as standard-bearer in high school; the last one of Ariel, which a comrade took of him in Río Gallegos before he left for the Malvinas; the one of Graciela receiving her diploma in Architecture; the one of Abelardo as godfather at Graciela's wedding, in her white gown, and holding him by the arm; the one of Abelardo at my side with the newborn Larisa in my arms; Larisa's graduation from high school ... A black hole remains where the shelf used to be. That's why some days I try hard to remember what their faces were like, their poses, their clothing, but the memories are fading, and I can't retain the traces of all of them, not even in my head.

I suggest that he eat part of the wall remaining behind my bed, instead; that way I don't always have to stare at what isn't there anymore. Because it's boring to lie there like that, especially before I fall asleep and after I turn off the TV, with my eyes always facing that hole, which grows bigger night after night. He doesn't say anything, because he never says anything, but then he looks at me through half-closed lids, and then I understand that, once again, he'll ignore me completely.

Since yesterday I've been putting the pillow at the foot of the bed, and I fall asleep looking at the wall behind the headboard, the one where the portrait of the Virgin hangs. I don't believe in the Virgin or saints or angels, but over time I've learned that whenever I say I'm an atheist, people grow uncomfortable, as if I were stabbing them in the ribs with a knife, so not only do I not mention it, but with some people, like Amanda, I let them think I'm a believer, because I know that way they'll feel most at ease. And now, well, I'm waiting for the cynocephalus to show up. I know that the change is going to surprise him and maybe even amuse him. And I'm anxious to see what the devil he'll do—if he's going to keep eating from the same wall, or if he'll change perspective, too. I also wonder what he'll think about a painting with that Virgin, draped in heavy, flowing robes, and that chubby little Botticelli Baby Jesus, and that angel with gray bird-feather wings.

The last time he was here, he ate up the sofa, so now he hunkers down on what little remains of the floor, at the edge of the blackness. When I get up at night to go to the bathroom, I have to be careful to put on my glasses and place my feet exactly where there's still a little bit of floor left in the room. Sometimes I imagine I'm about to take a misstep, or come to the very edge and fall into that void, the void that now practically surrounds me.

There's no more mirror or shower left in the bathroom. So today I asked Dora if she'd let me shower in her room. I told her I was having problems with the hot water and didn't want to catch pneumonia. She said yes. Dora's a very good person. And so I showered and changed, and now I'm back. With a lipstick in my hand, I walk over to the windowpane, where I see myself reflected, and I paint my lips pale pink.

Last night, while I was sleeping, I looked at what's left of the painting, which is part of the angel, an angel with the body and skin of a young man, with a face that now strikes me as very similar to Botticelli's own face, as lovely as a girl with those blonde corkscrew curls and those nearly-transparent eyes, and then those little wings with the gray feathers of a big, ugly bird emerging from his back. And I can't help wondering why most people don't find angels monstrous, though they would think of a cynocephalus as a monster. When I awoke, the angel and the section of wall where the remainder of the painting rested were no longer there. Then I took a sheet of paper and a pen from the nightstand and wrote the sign that I later stuck to the door with cellophane tape. I don't want anyone to carelessly come into the room and fall into the darkness.

Now I see him, standing by the bed, how he carefully takes off his jeans, then his shirt, his underwear, the clothes I gave him some time ago. I don't say anything to him; I just let him be.

He folds them methodically, placing one garment on top of another, on the quilt at the foot of the bed. He approaches on all fours, along the edge of the gorge that surrounds me, next to the darkness. He does this completely naked, the same as the first time, as I first met him. He sits on his haunches, puts one paw on the bed. I caress it. He moves his head forward, places his snout next to my hand. And, for some reason I can't quite comprehend, I know that he is saying goodbye. Everything around me is empty and dark now; the TV is silent. The bed looks phosphorescent, dressed in these white sheets and quilt in the midst of the blackness. The cynocephalus closes his eyes and prepares to fall asleep. I stick my hand under the pillow, take out the lipstick I've hidden there , and, before closing my eyes, I paint my lips so that when they find me, I will look beautiful.

SUBMERGED

Only those who have died are ours,
Ours is only what we have lost.
Jorge Luis Borges

AND THEN THAT noise wakes me with a start, a rough grinding that scrapes furiously against the hull of the boat. I must have fallen asleep on top of some tarps in the engine room, and the noise, which comes from outside but invades everything here on the inside, has awakened me. The noise multiplies, and now something at starboard scrapes, scratches, drags. I'm alone, there's no one in sight, it seems like everyone is where the noise is, or maybe everyone is the noise, as if the noise has swallowed them, the others, but not me, because

87

now I stand up and I'm fine, and I smooth my overalls with the palms of my slightly greasy hands, squat, grab the tarps, roll them up, and drag them out of the way. I've got to say that since that bout I had a few days ago, I'm feeling better, much better. The noise continues, but my ears are getting used to it and have started to distinguish other sounds, another reality beyond the noise: someone's coming in, someone who is still nothing more than the tapping of boots climbing down the metal ladder and touching the floor. I move toward the engine room door and determine that the someone is now a body that turns and comes toward the stern, a face that becomes more defined and takes on Soria's features: a nice guy, Soria, very good-natured. Then other boots: as the noise scrapes, scrapes, scrapes, now they're going down the ladder; then Soria stops, turns toward the guy behind him. When did they start? I think he's asking. A while ago, the other man replies with a voice that sounds like Albaredo's, as they complete their descent. And how do you get them off? Soria persists, with an intensity that struggles to be heard over the roaring, writhing, breaking din. With metal sheets, the other man explains as both of them advance toward the engine room. Argentine style, he adds, skin divers with snorkels, a metal sheet and lots of elbow grease, all by hand. The noise scrapes, scratches, grazes. Those barnacles are tough fuckers; they dig in real deep and they don't come off so easy, Albaredo explains. They haven't spotted me yet, I think, because Soria keeps asking: So what's the big hurry if they've been there for years? I dunno, the other one snaps back; there was an order and we gotta follow it. Now you can hear the clack of other boots, and still others, and other voices, and I go back to the engine room and stay there thinking about the barnacles clinging to the metal sheets as if they were the sheets themselves, adding excess weight to the boat and slowing it down, so slow, damaging the hull and making it unable to resist all the pressure it has to resist when it needs to dive deep, all because somebody had the bright idea of building that breakwater and didn't foresee that when the current changed, the submarine's hull would fill with those creatures. Neither did they plan ahead to bring it into dry dock for a proper cleaning, and who knows why it occurred to them just now to … The noise scrapes maddeningly, scrapes and scrapes and is deafening. The barnacles dig in like rabid dogs' teeth into living flesh, like the noise in my ears; they bite, they bite, they crunch. And bite.

The others have started to bring things aboard: provisions, boxes and cases with supplies, medicine, water, gasoline, tools, rocks, more rocks; they unload the practice torpedoes and load the ones for combat; the entire crew goes in and out, checks, arranges, puts things in order, cleans, and here I am, examining the engines again and again. This one's not working and isn't going to, suddenly announces Albaredo, who's working by my side, and those surrounding him grow nervous because they suspect something's going on, something beside the engines, the barnacles and the noise. Someone standing next to me remarks that today's paper mentioned some enormous whales near Punta Mogotes; it's a lie, someone else immediately adds, for sure it's a lie to distract people. From what? asks the one who spoke first; I dunno, the other guy responds, from something, how should I know, from this. I step outside the engine room, walk a few paces toward the control room, and from the bow I can see Estévez moving toward me, followed by two others, along the passageway that opens up between the bunks at port and starboard, toting a new broom, a bucket, some floor rags. The others carry a case of apples and a bag that looks like it holds potatoes or onions. Here, Gómez, this goes in your bunk, he must be saying to him as he hands Gómez the cleaning supplies with a smile that turns into an explosion of laughter. Gómez lays the things he's been given on the lower bunk while he finishes setting up his bed. Estévez and the two others with him continue down the passageway, bearing the case and the bag. Gómez stands there looking at them for a moment, checks his watch. Now Polski is approaching along the passageway between the bunks, his right hand clutching the handle of a zippered case that contains a small typewriter, and under his other arm a ream of paper. He's heading for the control room. I follow behind, and when he stops to readjust the typewriter and the paper, I pass him and continue toward the engine room. I decide to concentrate on the engines and on the work we're doing with Albaredo. Someone at the other end of the boat asks in a very loud voice if they've loaded on the jars of capers; I can't see him, but he's an officer, I say to myself, judging from the question and the tone of voice, and the noise picks up again with its racket: rrra, rrra, rrra, which doesn't let me hear the answer; though, really, what does the answer matter, what do we need capers for if the engine's screwed up? Rrra, rrra, rra, that noise ... What for, if that's going to make us spend more time snorkeling in order to charge the batteries? Rrra, rrra, rrra, rrrrra ... if that makes us more vulnerable, why the fuck do we need capers, rrra, rrra, rrrrra ... Something's going on, I know it, we all know it, even though no one says a thing, and for days now—I think, because I'm starting to lose count—for days I haven't moved from here. It's nighttime when they load on; I know it's nighttime because down here they turn on the night lights and the red ones in the control room to avoid reflections and to keep us from being seen from outside. Someone mentioned spies today; I heard him during a pause when the noise had stopped, Chilean spies, and someone else said no, they were North Americans who were staying in an apartment in one of the buildings on the other side of the avenue, opposite the base; Russians, someone else interrupted, they have to be Russians because the North Americans are on our side. Whatever, spies are spies, snoops holed up in an apartment from where they can watch all our movements; you can see movements on the base from anywhere; what a shitty location that base has. Now a different voice, from the periscope area, says: In the end everybody heard it on TV; nobody said anything before; but how is it possible that we have to find out about it on TV like everybody else. No one replies; everyone remains silent, me too, all the time thinking that anger is what's keeping us silent, so silent you can hear our breathing and even the momentary absence of the noise. Then someone who's climbing down the ladder at the bow, carrying boxes of crackers, points out that there's no moon tonight, that everything is black outside, completely black, perfect for hiding, for hiding what we're doing, what we're carrying, like well-trained little ants. The sea must also be black, I imagine, rhythmically black, and I start to feel sleepy again, the heavy sleepiness that suddenly takes hold of me, ever since my illness, dutifully forcing my eyes shut, till everything else goes black, too.

I don't know how much time has gone by since somebody said they learned what was going on from TV. The creaking noise has stopped, as if the sea has finally swallowed it up, and there's a dense, strained silence here that makes you think something is about to happen, something besides what already is silently happening. I'm alone again, so I make my way to the forward ladder. The hatch is open; I climb a couple of rungs to see what's going on outside, but a sticky fog hits me right in the face, in the eyes, like thick, cold mucus, and what I see is precious little: the others are standing in formation at the dock, a barely visible, dark blue stripe. What I don't understand is why the hell no one told me anything and I'm here in my work overalls; but anyway I make do with the little I can see and hear through the opening and the fog. That one over there is a priest, seems like: I bless you in the name of God, I bless you and pray for your safe return. Then it's true, we're weighing anchor and going on a mission, but not just any mission, the kind that rates a priest and a blessing. Now the Hyena's voice takes over; the Hyena is giving a speech, and even though I can't quite make out what he's saying, I'm sure he's talking to them with that permanent grimace of his that's not quite a smile or a tic or anything, just a frozen, nervous scowl. The Hyena was my commanding officer on our fifty-day campaign last year; every morning when he got out of bed, he put on a red bathrobe with a white silk handkerchief around his neck while he gave the raise periscope order to see what the day looked like and called for a cup of tea. Good hunting, the Hyena tells them, and suddenly the expression brings me back here from the past. After that, the others' boots click along the dock, the blue stripe stretches out into the fog, separates, melts into the darkness of falling night; they must be breaking rank and should be coming back on board. I go down the ladder; now I'm completely inside once more, not even time to say goodbye, what a shame, I would have liked to give María a hug, and my mother, too, but that's how things are these days; plenty of guys probably have gone through the same thing. I scramble all the way down to the bottom of the ladder and head for the engine room again. The fact is, I'm okay and I'm going to be part of this, whatever it may be. Now they're all coming down, the whole crew, each one is taking his place, Soria and Albaredo are also coming toward the engine room, Soria's very young, who knows what other guy's spot they've assigned him, some other machinist like me, of course, maybe it was urgent, because he's very young. Holding a broom in his hand, Soria laughs as he approaches, followed by Torres, who's laughing too. What's this, another broom? asks someone crossing in front of him; Oh, Soria replies, this is to attach to the sail when we get back, as a sign that the area's been swept. I'm worried about Diego, he's still got a fever—I think I recognize Almaraz's voice as he pokes his head out from the galley—I hope it's not anything out of the ordinary ... but then I lose track of his voice as it's swallowed up by the passageway, while Soria and Torres meet up with him on the way to the engine room, and now they're passing the Commanding Officer, who has a severe, concentrated look on his face, as if he'd aged ten years in the time it took for the blessing and the speech. They're negotiating, says a voice coming from the control compartment; they're negotiating and it's not going to come down to actual combat. Let's hope that's true, replies someone from the same location, because if not ... and suddenly the words get stuck in the intense rumbling of the engines that have just switched on: we're weighing anchor, we're on our way. My legs have hurt ever since the illness; if I stay still for very long my legs start to ache, so I take advantage of the fact that there's enough personnel in the engine room and decide to walk to the bow so I can move around a little, to see if the discomfort will go away. I cross the sonar area. Fuck me, Medrano is saying, why a priest if I'm not dead? I went for a walk around there till I saw that the priest was finished, says Medrano. Me, I just keep on moving forward through the periscope area; the CO isn't there anymore; I walk past the galley and in front of the CO's cabin, whose door is closed. I reach the rest area and then unintentionally hear Grunwald muttering in a lazy voice as he climbs up to his bunk: I was at a barbecue, goddamn it, right on Easter Sunday we had to set sail! At a barbecue, and I'm half-wasted, so now I'm going to bed and don't call me till I wake up, he says to me, I think, or maybe he says it to someone else, but anyway, another guy who's coming up behind me replies: They say he was granted leave to marry Old Lady Menéndez, that's why you're here. That son of a bitch could've gotten married later, Grunwald complains, covering himself with the sheet and yanking the little black corduroy curtain closed. I start walking again, continuing my route in order to stretch my legs, and I think about the fog on this Easter Sunday. Someone near the torpedoes confirms: They sent us to do drills, just drills, because we'll have to wait and see if the boat goes, if it responds or not; after all, the crew is new, lots of us don't even know each other; the CO doesn't know everyone, or the boat, either, and neither one of them, him or the Executive Officer, comes from a 209, and everything is different here. And on top of that, someone else adds, one of the four engines isn't working, it hasn't worked for years, the motor block is cracked. They'll work this thing out, someone else insists, they're gonna work it out diplomatically, that's why they started the whole thing, to yank the Brits' balls, but it'll all get worked out. Polski slips a cassette into the tape recorder in the control room, pushes a button, and over the loudspeaker—which is in the galley but can be heard throughout the boat—a military march blasts. I keep going forward, wrapped in the music, and immediately retrace my steps to the beat of the march, while I think about the fog that enfolds all of us, a dense fog I imagine as being solid gray, capable of hiding the outline of the submarine. Silver-white-gray hovering above the water, the sheltering fog that erases us as we head southward.

On the other side of the passageway, Soria makes his bed. Lying in my bunk, I watch him take the sheets out of his light-blue bag; they look coarse, stiff with that starch, that rubber sizing they have from the factory. It's a sure thing they didn't give him time to wash them, no way did they give him enough time, like so many of us. He's picked the top one, the third bunk from the bottom. He touches the mat; it probably feels damp. I had the same reaction when I went to lie down, but in fact it was cold; everything is cold here. Later on it'll be a little warmer, human warmth, the warmth of machines, too, of being enclosed. He unzips the mattress cover, a kind of envelope made of tightly woven sailcloth. He takes out the blanket and leaves it on the lower bunk. He flips the mattress over, adjusts it, slaps it gently with his open palms, spreads out the fitted blue sheet, navy blue, now the top sheet, also blue, but with stripes, some lighter, others darker, and every so often a very thin white one. He tucks one corner underneath the mattress, fastening it in place with a knot; it seems Soria doesn't like his sheets to come loose while he's sleeping. The thing is, he's very tall. He picks up the pillow, slightly sunken in the middle, exchanges it for the one on the lower bunk (he hasn't noticed I'm watching him; he must think I'm sound asleep), fluffs it a little with his hands, slips on the pillowcase and places it at the head of the bed. He takes the blanket he left on the lower bunk, unfolds it with a firm shake in the air, and spreads it over the mattress, smoothing out the fold lines, tucks in all the edges along the entire bunk bed. It's ready now. He picks up his bag again, rummages in his things till he finds his wallet, checks inside, pulls out a bill that looks like a fiver (judging from the color), folds it, and puts it back. He takes out a small photo, studies it intently, then looks upward. There's a slot: he wedges the photo in and stares at it for a few seconds; he seems satisfied. Now he pulls out a tape recorder, the kind with keys, and some boxes of cassettes, which he sets under his pillow. He pulls on the cords, closing the bag with the rest of his belongings inside, takes a few steps toward the lockers, opens the door to one of the cubbies and sticks the bag inside, squashing it a little toward the bottom and the back; he closes the door. Voices are approaching; you can hear laughter, too. Somebody announces that it's Monday, two-thirty. I pretend to be asleep so they won't say I've been spying, and in fact I don't want them to say anything. And I hear the order: we're diving; from now on we'll be traveling submerged.

For days now I haven't been able to find my boots. I've looked for them everywhere, but it's hopeless; just in case, though, I look under the bunks once more. Slightly toward the direction where the torpedo launchers end, Almaraz is writing in a little black notebook, in a very neat script; on the table beside him, there's a photo of a woman with a baby in her arms. I keep searching for my boots; no doubt someone hid them to play a gag on me, though it doesn't matter now—who wants to wear knee-high leather boots, only to get them covered with grease and walk around uncomfortably, making noise, on a submarine? Sometimes I think that someone on land, behind a desk, making decisions about clothing or so many other issues, tries really hard to screw us up because he's bored, as if all of us were part of a huge joke. When I think about those things, I can see the Hyena's smile: it follows me around, sticks to me, and it's hard for me to make it go away. Some people brought sneakers; others of us—like Soria and Heredia and Albaredo and so many more—walk around in our stocking feet, two or three pairs, one on top of the other, because it's starting to get cold in here now that we're submerged and are pretty far south. In the engine room socks get very dirty, everything gets dirty, full of grease, hardened by grime. On the other hand, the engines give off heat, more heat than they should, more than what's safe, and maybe we ought to be turning back to get them fixed, but the co said no, with the icy waters of the southern sea, that overheating will be balanced out. Even though the logical thing would've been to head north to intercept any subs or boats coming our way, we're going in the opposite direction, and for the time being, that's better for our engines. And so we keep navigating, paying a little more attention to the engines, more attention to the negotiations, as well, even though all we've had till now is silence. Most people say that this business will get straightened out and we'll go home soon, but nobody can be sure of it; nobody knows anything here; nothing is for sure. Uncertainty, that's the word—everything these days is uncertainty, except for the grime in the socks we're wearing.

When you're submerged the silence is complete, like deafness, like when a person has a bad cold and their ears are stopped up. We're all used to the permanent noise; that's why this sudden silence almost hurts. Until you get used to it, you have a strange feeling, like an empty space; then, little by little, your hearing returns to normal when it recovers the sounds of movement on board: voices, footsteps, the clanking of tools, the cook's pots crashing together. Just the same, it all ends up in a muffled din: if you're in the bunk area, you're close to the guys who are in the dining room, talking, but the sound hardly reaches you; it turns into a cottony murmur, even though the others are talking loudly. That's how things are in here.

There are times when I start thinking about food. I linger over the details of every dish I might eat, the colors, the exact flavor of every ingredient, but then, when it comes time to sit down at the table, I hardly eat a thing, nothing, really. Even though the food is good here, and the cook is excellent; but water is scarce, restricted, that's for sure; you have to be careful not to use it all up. Today the others had potato omelets and fish for lunch. I heard Almaraz say it was very good. This morning Almaraz complained of pain in his chest; he blamed it on the effort he made carrying things aboard on Saturday. The pain's not too bad, he explained, but it's annoying. He seems better now, though quite a few guys must have been thinking about my case: the terrible pain a few days ago that knocked me to the floor of the engine room. Of course I'm fine now and I've already forgotten about all that. Besides, I haven't felt the pain since. We're going to start cleaning the boat, you've got to do something, waiting isn't easy if you're not doing something concrete. We all get moving, each one heading for

98

the job he's been assigned. When I pass by the CO's cabin, I can see, through the little gap exposed by the half open door, that the nurse—standing against the curtain with those little yellow squares inside red squares that covers the shelves with our clothes—is taking his blood pressure. There's no doctor on board. A few steps beyond that, the cook is reading a D'Artagnan comic book, leaning against the galley counter. Grunwald goes to the head, for three days he's been running to the head again and again—to our head, the one for the petty officers—in spite of the charcoal that the nurse prescribed for him. We have one head for 28 petty officers, and there's one head for seven officers. The cook puts aside the D'Artagnan he was reading and picks up another comic that he's now starting to read. Grunwald comes out of the head, his face pale, and retreats down the passageway toward the bow, swearing softly. We may all be characters in a ridiculous comic strip.

I guess it's dawn because we're rising to periscope depth in order to snorkel. The sub is rocking, the sea must be rough on the surface; the sub veers from port to starboard, and immediately you can hear the noise of things falling, rolling, crashing, breaking, some glasses, maybe cups that weren't stowed away in the galley. In the half-light of nighttime, the first mate gets up to see what's happened. Suddenly I hear him grumble and swear; then I peek out from my bunk and see him lift his foot, maybe the right one, and grab his toes. The nurse, who also has gotten up because of the noise, goes to him and checks him out. I'm very drowsy and go back to sleep.

I've just finished my shift and leave the engine room for my bunk. On the way there I see the CO walking from the first periscope to his cabin. I take a few steps down the narrow passageway behind him, and when he reaches his cabin he suddenly turns around to go back the way he came. I stand aside to let him pass and take up my course again. I watch him go back and see that when he reaches the first periscope, he turns again to return to his cabin. I lower my eyes; it makes me uncomfortable to think that he may have caught me watching him, and so I continue walking toward the bunks as the CO once more arrives at his cabin, no doubt with the intention of turning yet again and walking back to the periscope. Standing in front of my bed, I discover that someone is lying in it. That happens sometimes, so I climb up to the top one, which is empty. Meanwhile I see Soria arrive, climb up, and collapse in his own bunk, at the same level as the one I'm in now, but on the opposite side of the passageway. I rearrange the pillow and lie down. Soria lies down too, and now he stretches his arm up in the air. There must be some 40 centimeters between him and the ceiling; everything is narrow here, compressed, and he's passing his hand over the little photo he had placed in the slot. Forty centimeters to the ceiling, and then, tons of icy water, tons of ocean above my head, above the heads of the others, above the head of the CO as he comes and goes from the first periscope to his cabin and from his cabin to the first periscope, everyone under tons of water. I never stopped to think about this in spite of all the time I've been a submariner, never until now, maybe because now everything seems to be different. So much endless water out there, so many things together in the narrow space of this tube. The fluorescent lights go out, the night navigation lights go on. If not for that, it would be impossible to tell: there's no day or night in here.

The little black curtain of the bunk beneath Soria's moves: someone is opening it, he stands up and consults his watch: it's Heredia, it must be time for his shift, they're probably going to take advantage of the night to rise to snorkel altitude and do the venting. Heredia climbs out of his bunk, straightens the sheets a little, zips the case shut to cover everything, picks up the crate of apples that's sitting on the lower bunk and places it on his bunk. For a moment he stands there looking at the fruit, and so do I, some of them wrapped in delicate, purple paper, others unwrapped, red and shiny, crossed by a few green streaks. And Heredia emerges slowly, walking toward the torpedo area. Apples, apples, one on top of another, next to one another, under one another, apples in an apple crate. We're rising now; I can feel it in my body. Besides, the apple crate has slid a few centimeters sternward.

They're playing *truco* on the aft table. Almaraz is writing in his little black notebook again, someone is drinking coffee, Polski smiles as he draws a cartoon of one of us on a piece of paper with the shield of the Argentine Navy. I pass behind the benches, circling around them, and suddenly I think I see— underneath the curtain separating the table from the bunks at stern, which we call the red light district—the tips of my boots. I think they're my boots because one of them has a small, dark, curved nick at the tip, which I made some time ago. I don't say anything. Either someone is playing a gag on me or else I must have left them there by mistake, because it was in this section that I fell asleep during the previous campaign. And yet I remember looking for them and not seeing them. Or maybe I just think I looked for them, but I only meant to,

I don't know: lately I've been getting things mixed up; it's as if facts and thoughts have the same weight, as if everything is consistent, but at the same time slippery. No matter: just in case this was only a gag, I carefully pick up the boots and don't say anything; once more I pass behind the card players and silently walk back to my bunk, placing them on top of it— resting against one of the edges of the bed—and I cover them with the blanket I sometimes use to cover my feet.

For a few days now we've had a certain noise; it comes from above, probably from someplace between the hull and the deck. When the sub rolls, the noise begins: taka-taka-taka, taka-taka-taka, tak, and then taka-taka-taka, taka-taka-taka, but we don't know what causes it. Then it suddenly disappears and we don't hear it again and we go on doing our usual thing. Today is clothes-changing day, and since we need to save water, the clothes aren't washed, so all of us put our dirty stuff in a bag and someone adds rocks, too, the rocks that were loaded on board specifically to act as ballast when they throw the filled bags out the garbage ejector at the stern. Nobody wants them to float to the top for the Brits to discover, so that's why the rocks, to leave our dirty rags at the bottom of the sea. Taka-taka-taka, taka-taka-taka, here comes the noise again. I hope someone will decide to do something, though surfacing at a time like this would mean revealing our presence, taka-taka-taka, taka-taka-taka-tak. The noise, that noise—sooner or later it's going to give us away.

I watch Soria and Torres work; for days now they've been wearing their life jackets all the time. A submariner's life jacket has its special features: an inflatable part that goes around the neck, and on the chest a metal sheet under which there's a bottle with gas that's used to fill up the inflatable part, in addition to a series of straps and loops to adjust it to the body. Well, it's obvious this isn't exactly the most comfortable thing in the world. All day and all night Torres and Soria wear their life jackets for doing their work as machinists, for eating, for sleeping, for taking a shit. They're afraid, though if not for the life jackets, nobody would notice their fear because they keep doing what they have to do like the rest of us. Now they're calling us to our stations; it's a drill so that we'll be prepared in case the day comes when we really do have to man the battle stations. I see Olivero pass behind Marini, who's standing in front of the fire control computer; Olivero advances, his head hanging, maybe as a precaution to avoid exchanging looks with Marini in case he should accidentally turn around. Ever since we started the campaign they haven't been talking to each other; they were always good friends, but now they avoid one another all the time. Something must have happened between them. Marini sits down in the computer operator's seat; we all occupy our stations, Torres and Soria with their life jackets on their backs. The tension has grown, you can tell by certain gestures; I, on the other hand, feel fairly calm even though I can't really explain why.

Beards have grown, nobody shaves; we're surrounded by water but there *is* no water, not for shaving; there's no reason to shave, either, no motivation, no one to do it for. That's why they all go around scratching themselves; a beard itches when it starts to grow, it itches a lot for a few days; later you get used to it and the hair grows and stops itching. That time will come soon, and by then we'll surely have our hands—and our minds—

busy with other things. All of us bearded, except Soria, who's too young, so young that his whiskers haven't even started to grow yet.

A muffled sneeze, barely audible, though there are two or three guys with colds, since it's very cold in here. Judging from the nearness of the sound, I imagine it must be Cuéllar. I poke my head out of the engine room; Cuéllar blows his nose gently to avoid making noise, Medrano, who's sitting in front of the sonar, gestures, and Cuéllar approaches, Medrano whispers something to him and hands him his earphones, Cuéllar puts them on, listens attentively for a few moments, nods, returns the earphones to Medrano, and while Medrano continues to listen, Cuéllar takes broad, but quiet, steps toward the control room and explains something to the communications officer; he must have told him they've detected noise on the hydrophones because immediately they call us to our battle stations, and so I return to the engine room. We're in a permanent safe zone, in our patrol area, just one hundred miles from the exclusion zone, and we all know that this is no drill: for the first time in our lives, this call to the battle stations is absolutely real. Maybe it's a sub, says Soria, huddled in his life jacket; it has to be English if it's circling around here, Torres adds from inside his; none of our ships are in this zone. I look out toward the sonar section and see Medrano making signs. Then someone turns off the fans to eliminate even the tiniest sound, and suddenly there's a void that seems to be sucking up everything except this new deep, desperate silence. Possibly a freighter, Medrano whispers to the communications officer. All of us standing close enough to hear look at one another; no one utters a word, no one moves. Cuéllar presses his handkerchief to his nose; a sneeze right now would be unfortunate. Soria adjusts the buckles on his life jacket, Torres copies his movements, I stare at the black grease stains on the toes of my socks. Almaraz directs his gaze to the oxygen meter, Polski grips the horizontal rudder he's operating. Freighter withdrawing, sir, Medrano announces—in a soft, but confident voice—a few eternal seconds later. We breathe, we calm down, though just a little because we remain in silence, a cautious, superstitious silence, till Medrano confirms that the sounds on the hydrophone have stopped. Not until then do we take a deep breath, our bodies loosen up, our faces relax. The cook brings coffee to the sonar technicians, saying have some coffee, boys, and he hands over the two pitchers with a smile. Medrano and Cuéllar thank him, look at one another, clink the pitchers together, satisfied, toasting, and we all begin to move around, each one doing his own thing, nothing happened, not this time. The nurse comes by with his first aid kit; I follow him with my eyes to see what's going on. Nothing, apparently; he chats with the Executive Officer, who gets up from his chair at the control table and heads for the officers' cabins, followed by the nurse. I decide to go back to my bunk for a handkerchief, I think I may have caught cold, too; when I pass by the officers' cabins, the half-open door allows me to see that the Executive Officer has removed his right sock, and he's having another treatment. I continue on my way to my bunk to get the handkerchief and I see that my boots have disappeared; the blanket I use to cover my feet is neatly folded, just like the day we set sail and I made my bed, folded in thirds in that special way I do it, just as if the boots had never been there. I run my hand over it to make sure of what at first glance seems obvious, confirming their absence. I can't try to look for them now; it's my shift in the engine room, I'll do it when I'm done. I take the handkerchief I keep under the pillow, it's damp but I blow my nose anyway, I adjust the pillow, which also feels damp, the sheets are damp, the blankets are damp, the towels, clothing, socks, skin, tools, the dry crackers, everything's damp in here. I stick the handkerchief in my pocket and walk to my post next to the engines; I cross paths with the nurse, who has finished the Executive Officer's treatment and is now on his way to the galley. Someone asks Almaraz about the pain in his chest. Almaraz replies that the pain has gone away and that he feels okay. I continue on my way to the engine room; a drop suddenly falls on the middle of my head from a manifold above: even our breath condenses and rains down on us. When I pass by the control room, someone mentions that there are problems with the fire control computer; I see an officer sitting next to Marini, both of them at the keyboard. I pass through the control compartment, arrive at the engine room. Soria looks at me without seeing me; a heavy, slow drop of water breaks off from the lower buckle of his life jacket and starts to fall and will keep on falling till it bursts, if nobody gets in its way, right on the tip of the sock on his right foot.

It's Sunday, somebody says, which means it's already been a week since we weighed anchor. We've had no communications or news, we don't know what's happening outside. Today the technicians were working on the computer again, it seems there are operational problems that prevent us from calculating the torpedo launches precisely, leaving us helpless and hopelessly ridiculous. My shift is over, and before going off to take a nap, I go on a quest to recover my boots; I decide to return to the bunks in the red light district to see if someone has hidden them there again; it doesn't seem likely they would choose the same place, but I can't think of where else to begin, and so that's where I'm going. There are noises in the galley, I peek in through the open door and see them, Almaraz and Polski, opening a couple of boxes of powder, one of them preparing to make cakes, the other cracking eggs, both of them standing before an enormous metal bowl. Now Polski uses a spoon to pry open the cover of the tin of powdered milk that sits on the counter, then—spoonful by spoonful—he transfers the white powder to a plastic measuring cup with lines to indicate measurements, adds water, stirs. Almaraz takes a huge pot from the pantry and places it on a burner. Now Polski beats the milk with the rest of the preparation. Almaraz greases a large mold, turns on the oven, dumps cocoa powder into the pot, adds several measures of powdered milk, a few tablespoons of sugar, then enough water to combine, stirs, lowers the flame under the pot, while Polski pours the batter into the greased mold and puts it in the oven. I continue walking toward the bow; there are a few people gathered there, playing *truco* again. At the same table Olivero writes something on some papers, concentrating hard; he writes and crosses out and writes again. Heredia asks them to let him know when they're done, as Polski has put him in charge of cleaning and setting the table. I take advantage of the situation to slip unnoticed behind those who are sitting around the table, and suddenly I see them, in the same spot where I found them last time, both boots, their tips barely visible beneath the bunk's drawn curtains. What a stupid joke, I say to myself, and suddenly the dark groove at the tip of the left boot reminds me—I don't know why—of the Hyena's grimace. We're on a mission, sailing in the Lemere Canal, near the Picton Islands, at that time in conflict with Chile; it's very shallow where we are, and the sonar tech reports that he can hear noise on the hydrophones that he thinks is a launch. The Hyena is the commanding officer and he's taking us to a place where we shouldn't be, so shallow that if it does turn out to be one of the Chilean torpedo boats patrolling the strait, it could destroy us even if it launched candies. At the sonar tech's warning, the Hyena's face wrinkles up, he turns even paler than usual, we all see the fear on his face and the fact that he doesn't know what to do. Like every other day, he's wearing his red bathrobe with the white scarf around his neck, acting for all the world like a German submarine captain from the Second World War. Suddenly, to our collective relief, the sonar tech announces: Sir, I classify the contact as a crabbing launch or a fishing boat. Then he half-collects himself and orders the periscope raised to confirm what the sonar tech petty officer has just announced, immediately followed by the order to lower periscope at full speed because the launch is getting closer, closer, it starts to pass over us, very nearby, continues on its way, still above us, till it passes by, starts moving away, away; we were lucky, that's all, just a bit of luck. A few hours later, now out of the strait, we emerge: the Hyena, in his red robe and white scarf, peers out of the sub's sail with a pair of binoculars. I stand there watching him as if all that were happening right now; suddenly a fog begins to cover him, a fog thick enough to hide his loud bathrobe and his bright scarf, though not solid enough to conceal his smile, which is now a laugh, a thunderous burst echoing inside the dark dent in my left boot. My boots! I grab the boots, I don't know how much time has passed, sometimes I'm not fully aware of that, time turns elastic here, it goes by quickly or stops indefinitely, but the fact is that now the others have finished their card game and are gathering the cards together, tidying the table. Olivero picks up his papers, covered with strikeouts, folds them, and stores them, together with the ballpoint pen, in his jacket pocket; Heredia has returned from the galley with a damp dishrag, waiting for everybody to finish so he can start wiping down the table. Since they're busy, I use their distraction to remove my jacket and wrap up my boots in it, and I slip away to my bed, wondering why the hell I'm so concerned with getting my boots back if I don't wear them, if the joke is just an innocent detail in the midst of all we've living through, but there I go, making my way down the corridor, boots in hand. When I pass by the galley, Polski is taking the sponge cake out of the oven, Almaraz has put the pot on the countertop and is stirring the steaming chocolate with a wooden spoon, no doubt to avoid forming that kind of skin the milk forms on the surface when it cools. I keep moving till I reach my bed, where I lay the package with the boots, looking both ways as I think about where to hide them; two or three of the others are sleeping in their bunks; from one of them, behind the little corduroy curtain, you can hear Torres' voice whispering, I'll bet he's recording a cassette for his girlfriend; Torres has a little tape recorder, half the size of the one Soria uses for listening to music; Soria's always making jokes about that, telling Torres—referring to their tape recorders—that they're father and son. I see Polski coming along toward the control room; I pretend to be straightening out the blanket and the jacket; Torres keeps talking to his girlfriend as if she were here, recording words he knows there's no way she'll receive. Polski returns with a sheet of lined paper and goes into the galley again; no one's coming, so I take the jacket with the boots and head for the engine room. Now there are four men hunched over the fire control computer; it looks like they can't figure out the problem and this is a big, scary deal. In the engine room Soria and Albaredo are busy with one of the engines and don't even notice me, so I go ahead and hide my boots behind the convertor. When I leave the engine room, I see that the co has joined the group around the computer, so I keep on going and run into the Executive Officer, who's also headed there. Before joining this boat, the XO was chief engineer on the Santiago del Estero; one time I visited that sub because the bubble on ours was broken, and they sent me there to get the part because they had one on the Santiago del Estero. I go below, and when my eyes grow accustomed to the interior of the sub, I see people gathered in the periscope area; I start to move forward, but someone breaks away from the group, takes a couple of steps toward me and arrogantly says, Hey, you, what are you looking for? I try to explain, but he cuts me off before I can finish and says: Wait here, someone will help you. Now Maceda is the XO on this boat and he's going toward the fire control computer. I try to be positive, not to worry, if each one does a good job with what he has to do ... Then I sneeze and taka-taka-taka, taka-taka-taka-tak, again that damn noise, maybe I'll go to the galley and get something hot, a nice cup of coffee will do me good, and then I'll lie down to rest because by the time I remember, it'll be my shift again. I leave the jacket on the bed and set out for the galley, the cake that was in the oven just a while ago now rests on a tray. I stand there, watching how Polski frosts it with *dulce de leche* and now he writes HAPPY BIRTHDAY NOBREGA with thick blue marker on a sheet of office paper, which a few minutes earlier he had brought to the galley from the control room, making a cone with it and pressing it into the thick frosting layer on the cake. He carries the tray with the cake on it toward the multi-use table in front of the torpedo area. I turn my eyes toward the galley counter in search of the coffeepot; with a large spoon, Almaraz is completing the process of pouring the hot chocolate into some cups on a tray; now he carefully picks up the tray and leaves. Heredia walks in, drops the dishrag in the sink, and walks out again, most likely also on his way to the bow. I decide it would be better not to take anything, the coffee will just keep me awake, so I leave the galley and for a few seconds I stand there in the doorway, hesitating, not quite knowing what to do. At the bow someone is giving out cups of hot chocolate; you can hear laughter; I finally head back to my bunk; someone else emerges from the galley carrying cider and glasses; I climb up into my bed and from there I can hear them being served, now they're singing Happy birthday, happy birthday Nobrega, and many more, applause, some howling, the crowd is celebrating, spirits are high today after what happened yesterday, and I'd like to be a part of it, I'd like to be there, too, but I'm exhausted, with a weariness that drags me toward the dark pit of sleep. I look forward again, the others are posing for pictures, squeezed together around the table, somebody yells *whiskey*, then a click, applause, more laughter. I lie down just as I am; I don't even feel like getting undressed; Torres has finished talking to his girlfriend and is coming down from his cot, still wearing his life jacket; Soria's coming, also bundled up in his life jacket, he leaves the engine room and goes into the petty officers' head; Torres walks over to the table where everyone is celebrating. I close my eyes and lose contact with my surroundings.

Now that the festivities seem to have ended, a uniform murmur reaches me from the bow: some people are praying, maybe because it's Sunday, maybe because they're lonely, maybe because they're afraid. I don't pray, not even from here, from bed, I don't know why, but today I can't, my voice doesn't work, not even that quiet inner voice people use for praying.

I've just climbed into my bunk and see that Polski, standing next to his, is preparing one of those towels they supply us with before we set sail, the ones with a blue anchor printed on them, I suppose to remind us that we're in the Navy. Today is bath day, though around here bathing is just a figure of speech, an expression whose meaning is quite different from what it means to outsiders. Here water is conserved, you have to use it sparingly, the distillers don't work right: they use a lot of energy and, besides, they make a terrible racket. Polski's towel is new, just like the others; new means waterproof, with a layer of sizing, or paraffin, or I don't know what, in any case something that will keep it from absorbing a single drop of water—at least for a good, long time. Polski starts to undress beside his bunk, tugging at his sneakers to take them off, a pair of sporty sneakers that he bought himself to keep from making noise when he walks; then he takes off his left sock and, after dropping it on top of one sneaker, he pulls off the right one and drops it on top of the other sneaker. Next, his pants, standard-issue navy blue cloth—first one leg, then the other—now turned a kind of dark, grayish black, with all sorts of stains, like the pants and overalls of the rest of the crew. Then the blue shirt, which he rolls up into a ball, leaving it on the bunk, and the undershirt, the "elastic," as it's called around here, with a double layer of flannel at chest level; he wraps the towel around his waist and slips off his undershorts beneath, maybe his first change of underwear in several days, of those shorts provided by the Navy, the "regulation" ones, stiff with sizing or elastic, hard like the towel, capable of causing the most uncomfortable irritation you can imagine. He makes a knot in the towel, and then holds it closed with his hand, just in case some joker—and there's no lack of those—should yank it off, leaving him buck naked. With his free hand he picks up some soap, a brush, and toothpaste and proceeds toward the petty officers' head. The red, night navigation lights flash on, and for a second it reminds me of a cheesy nightclub, the scene makes me laugh, and I turn over to get ready to sleep. Right under the head door is the air conditioning equipment; if Polski has to wait because someone is in there, he'll freeze his ass off. Then he'll go inside, of course, shivering a little, or a lot, he'll close the door because if he doesn't he won't be able to shower, since the shower is right behind the door and in front of the metal toilet full of handles and levers that serve to eject toward the tank whatever gets dumped in there. But Polski isn't really going to shower, there's not enough water for every man to take a shower, and so once he's inside the head, he'll leave the door half-open, undo the knot in his towel, and—sticking his hand through the narrow opening he's left—he'll hang the towel from the low-pressure air manifold out in the passageway, to avoid putting it down in the limited head space that so many others have already used today (there's no room in there for a towel that never dries); then he'll close the door and turn to the left in order to face the sink—stuck right in there—with its stainless steel mirror that barely allows him to recognize himself in it, partly because it's all scratched, partly because of the beard he's been growing, and maybe because after a while

113

you stop recognizing yourself and don't even want to see your reflection. Standing in front of the sink, he'll press down on the valve and put his cupped, hollowed palms underneath to catch the water that comes out, and right after that he'll wash his face, to refresh himself and also to rinse off a little of the routine or discouragement or sleepiness or fear, depending on whichever happens to apply to the "bather." Then he'll repeat the routine, the steps necessary to use another little bit of water, and he'll wash his arms, his armpits, with soap. Once more he'll maneuver to catch the water in his hands, and he'll splash it over himself to rinse off, and again fill his hands to aim straight for his dick, and then his asshole, and then his feet, raising one, then the other, gathering water, dampening himself, soaping, gathering water, rinsing, lots of patience, lots of skill, lots of maneuvers, lots of balance. Then he'll half open the door, stick out his hand, and grope for the towel from the manifold to dry himself with, or in any case to distribute the water up and down his whole body, still slightly damp, slip back to his bunk, the undryable towel rolled around his waist, to put on new underwear, clean and white, tugging on it a little to force it over his too-damp skin. And after Polski, someone else will go in to "bathe," and another, and another; and that's how it'll go all night and all day. Somebody asks, no doubt peeking into the galley, what's for dinner today? Pizza and steak with tomatoes, the cook's voice replies, and for dessert, torta Balcarce with meringue. I stay where I am, all curled up with my back to the passageway, not eating, not bathing, and still unable to catch a wink of sleep.

We're in a deep sea channel, a bubble of water that's even colder than the already-cold water we've been sailing in; the engines have been turned off and the sub floats gently, following the current, with us inside, and that way it becomes undetectable; sounds bounce off the thermal barrier of the channel and it's as if it didn't exist, as if it had suddenly become water, all water: the boat, us, objects, time, just water in the water.

From my bunk I see the row of four, of those that are on the other side of the passageway, diagonally across from mine: in the lower one, Bighead Cuéllar is opening his Bible, a small Bible he carries with him on all the campaigns; in the bunk right above his, Helmsman Navarrete is resting; above him, Linares, and in the last one, the one closest to the ceiling, there's someone, but from here I can't make out his features; judging by the skinny body and the sneakers peeking out from beneath the blankets, it looks like Egea, the waiter, who, ever since we weighed anchor on this trip has always gone to bed fully dressed and with his sneakers on. Rest easy, you guys, Cuéllar reassures them in a whisper, I'm going to pray for us, all four of us in this row, so nothing will happen to us. Then he opens his Bible and reads, with the gentle intonation of prayer: *Now the Lord provided a huge fish to swallow Jonah, and Jonah was in the belly of the fish three days and three nights. From inside the fish Jonah prayed to the Lord his God. He said: You hurled me into the depths, into the very heart of the seas, and the currents swirled about me; all your waves and breakers swept over me. When my life was ebbing away, I remembered you, Lord, and my prayer rose to you, to your holy temple. Those who cling to worthless idols turn away from God's love for them. But I, with shouts of grateful praise, will sacrifice to you. What I have vowed I will make good. I will say, "Salvation comes from the Lord." And the Lord commanded the fish, and it vomited*

Jonah onto dry land.

A couple of the guys bring out the whip antenna and listen. There's a group of men gathered around the radio, all wanting to know how the negotiations are going, if there's any news; sometimes they get Radio Colonia and manage to catch some information. Those who are listening gossip among themselves, hands on hips, now somebody breaks away from the group, walks along the passageway by the bunks and remarks—nervously scratching his overgrown beard—that Chile seems to be prepared to assist the Brits. Now I see him, the guy that just announced this news, retracing his steps and heading for the fire control computer, maybe with the intention of lending a hand to see if he can fix it, but that computer can't be fixed, not with the equipment we've got here; the logical thing would be to turn back toward Comodoro to get it fixed, but for now we're not moving, we're waiting for orders, and— most of all—hoping that the enemy won't find us. Against all foreseeable predictions, we've been ordered to stay right where we are until further notice, so we'll have to get along without a computer. And what about those guys who were in Germany, with their families, perfecting their knowledge of this kind of equipment for the 209, where are they? Not here. They never boarded this boat, maybe they were there that foggy day when we embarked, waving from the docks, but now, right now, when we need them, they're not here. We'll have to calculate the launching manually, like in the Second World War, by hand, and one torpedo at a time, instead of two or three, launching torpedoes we've never tried before. Suddenly the Hyena's smile appears before me, floating in the air, just his smile, separated from the face it belongs to, like some stupid ad for toothpaste, but instantly it disappears and I feel overcome by this stubborn exhaustion I've been lugging around lately. Voices reach me from the computer area, several different ones, arguing about something I can't quite hear, or don't want to hear. So I decide to go back to the bunks and get into bed, plunge into my damp, cold, deep sea channel, my water bubble, so I can become invisible for a few hours.

We've been snorkeling now for a long time; several of the others are gathered around the periscope and the masts because that's where the sea air, the fresh air, gets in; a few of them are smoking; all of them, those who smoke and those who don't, look upward even though you can't see anything, just feel the damp, icy, penetrating air of this sea against your face; I'm standing close by. Navarrete approaches, too, and remarks that they're not receiving signals on the radar screen, so they're going to retract the antenna to see what's happening. There's tension: whenever we snorkel, the sub becomes vulnerable, easier to spot, and besides, we have no radar now, which is one of the pieces of equipment that allow us to spot the enemy. They lower the antenna; some of the smokers move aside, Navarrete and Marini come over with tools and start checking it; it seems the receiver is broken. Even though it's not time for my shift yet, I decide to go to the engine room to see what they're doing, but no sooner do I take a couple of steps than a song hits me; in spite of the low volume, I think I recognize the voice of Joan Manuel Serrat—*Which of my many loves will buy flowers for my funeral?*—the voice grows louder as I approach, *Who will take care of my dog?*, and now, as I reach the control compartment, I run into Soria, who's sitting in the helmsman's seat, opposite Polski and Almaraz, each one in his seat at the horizontal rudders. *Who will pay for my burial and a metal cross?* On his knees, like a curled-up cat, Soria has his little tape recorder with its colored keys that reproduces the Catalonian singer's voice, *Who will lie down in my bed, wear my pajamas, and support my wife?* Damn, I say to myself, it's as if the guy was here among us saying what we're all thinking, *Who will that good friend be, the one who'll die with me, even a little?* Polski draws spirals on his thigh with his index finger, on top of the wrinkled cloth of his blue pants; Almaraz adjusts the beret he's wearing today and strokes his beard; Soria moves the little metal extension on one of the open buckles of his life jacket up and down; *Who will finish my diary* ... all three of them listen silently, ... *when the last page falls from my calendar?* Some voices come up behind me; I turn toward the control room, the radar screen is registering signals, it seems they were able to fix the antenna, there's no enemy in sight, the helmsman comes and occupies his place, the snorkel operation is over and we're going to total immersion. Soria presses the black key, turns off his tape recorder, and stands, but the song still repeats in my head: *Who will finish my diary . . .? Which will be the last page on my calendar?*

I dream about Mancuso, Mancuso from the *Santa Fe.* He looks tired, very tired, with rage or worry; we did a few campaigns together and I know how his face looks when things aren't going well. Someone's coming, he's coming in through the battery hatch at the stern, not one of our guys, he has a weapon in his belt and he stops a few feet away from Mancuso; the intruder's eyes are too blue, and it seems like he's watching him. It's a silent dream, I can't detect any sound at all, and that makes it terribly annoying. Suddenly the sub lists, Mancuso jumps up and starts to open one of the valves at port to avoid a disaster, but just then I see him slump over abruptly. The guy who isn't one of ours looks at his drawn weapon in shock, two other guys show up in the same crisp uniforms as the one with the weapon, but I don't see them anymore, just Mancuso's face, lying on his side on the floor, with a grimace of rage, as if he had asked a question that no one will ever answer.

I dream about Marini, our fire control computer operator. I see him swimming, swimming desperately in a stormy sea, beside a brightly colored fishing boat, he paddles, picks up momentum, and dives, once more emerges, paddles, picks up momentum and dives again, as if he's looking for someone, and so on for a time that feels maddening, eternal, to me, because I can see him from here but can't do anything to help him. And then his arms no longer appear emerging from the water, I can't see him anymore, only the sea, the sea, and the tiny boat whose colors slowly fade from my view.

I don't know why I have these dreams that sometimes don't seem like dreams, it's as if I was living them, as if I could momentarily access another time and another place, as if all that was real, too.

I dream about Polski: I'm standing on a broken-up stretch of sidewalk and I see him driving a taxi; I motion for him to stop, I want to say hello, and besides, I urgently need for him to take me someplace, though I don't yet know where, but he doesn't stop, it's as if he doesn't see me, as if I'm not there, but I run after him anyway, I shout out his name and run behind the car for a couple of blocks, but in the end I lose sight of him down some dark little streets on the outskirts of Mar del Plata.

I dream again about Polski driving a taxi, but this time

when the dream starts I'm inside the taxi; he's picked me up as a passenger, but I have the feeling he doesn't recognize me, I give him an address and he seems to nod in agreement, but after a few blocks I see that he's taking a different route and we're going, going, going, never stopping, not braking, not accelerating, as if the car was mounted on a conveyor belt: I look down and see that I'm wearing my boots, I'm absorbed, staring at the dent in the left toe, as we keep on going, till I lift my head and realize that we're approaching the cemetery. Polski stops the car, turns around toward the passenger seat and sees me, he sees me and I understand that he knows who I am; we're here, he announces. But I don't want to get out of the taxi, not at a cemetery I didn't ask to be taken to. And so I stay there, just looking down, absorbed by the dent in the tip of my boot, which is growing deeper, deeper and warmer and finally cozy.

Sometimes I dream of a circus, with a tent all made of more and more triangles of brightly-colored canvas, and edged with thousands of little electric lights; I dream, as if seeing all that from the air, flying over it. There's some land behind the circus, and on it a cage with an enormous Bengal tiger that always paces from one side to the other, in a back-and-forth that falsely expands the space he doesn't have, and, as I float a little lower and closer now, I see Grunwald, too, walking over to the cage and talking to the tiger as if the tiger was a person and could understand him, he talks to him and through the bars he offers him a huge chunk of meat; then the tiger approaches with his heavy, but silent, steps, stretches out his neck, brings his head over to the bars, spreads his jaws and bites the meat: Grunwald screams, it's an automatic, piercing scream that lasts as long as it takes for him—also automatically—to pull his hand away, now bleeding and missing the thumb. Grunwald curses as he rips off his tee shirt and wraps the wound, and then I see it peeking out from underneath his tee shirt, creeping and obvious against his skin, a black line that grows and rises quickly, quickly, as though time were speeding up, it climbs up his arm without stopping, and I begin to fall in a spiral toward a void, also black, where nothing more remains: neither Grunwald nor the tiger nor the colored triangles of the circus tent, nor the little electric lights, nor me.

Other times I dream that someone, who I can't identify because I see him from behind, is moving around the Navy Petty-Officers School of Mechanics at night, groping, half-naked, as if just out of bed, the skinny body of a teenager gropes his way as though looking for something. Then he reaches a door, tries to open it but can't, turns a little to his right and continues walking close to the wall; suddenly he stops, places his ear against the wall and listens, moves away, looks toward the door, comes back to rest his ear again, as if his extreme attention might scratch the wall in search of the echo of a voice or maybe a repeated moan; he listens once more. Now he quickly returns to the door, turns the doorknob in vain, the door won't yield, he shakes it; he wants to get out of there, it seems, but the door remains closed, the lights go on, and the boy stands there quietly, petrified, his eyes fixed on the floor; the officer in charge of the school comes toward him, jostles him: you're asleep, you're sleepwalking, cadet, go back to bed and don't let it happen again. Two other officers appear out of nowhere and take him away, subdued. Then I wake up and think I hear footsteps, but there's no one walking here, it's the bilge pump that keeps making noise and I can't go back to sleep.

A group, larger this time, is gathered around the radio, there must be six or seven of them, packed in tight, trying to find out how things are going outside. I imagine they couldn't possibly be worse: I have the strange feeling we're alone. Somebody raises an arm with a closed fist, shaking it as though he's celebrating something. Soria goes over to him and asks him a question, whispering in his ear, then he comes over and says—I don't know if he's talking to Albaredo or to me but it doesn't matter—that an English helicopter fell into the water and a petty officer has died. Some people smile, happy, and I wonder if it's good or bad, given the state of things, that an English helicopter has fallen into our sea. I turn around and head for the galley; maybe—to the English, anyway—the death of a petty officer doesn't matter much. Now I'm walking past our head, the one for the petty officers, and I see Torres waiting outside because the head is occupied; he scratches his scalp, poor Torres, he must be struggling to hold it in because it's his bad luck to be a petty officer and have to share the head with 27 others like him. I reach the galley and look for a little juice; the nurse is at the counter helping himself to some coffee. Lieutenant Rabellini walks in, rubbing the back of his neck, he says something about a terrible headache, then the nurse leaves his full pitcher on the counter and walks away, going for his satchel, I imagine, because Rabellini follows him. In the end I give up looking for the juice and return to the engine room. Torres is still waiting outside our head while the officers' toilet is unoccupied.

Today several of the others are standing around the radio again, all of them silent, leaning over the device waiting for some news from outside. One of them straightens up, turns around, and says something about the English landing at South Georgia Island. Faces change, shrink: this time there's no turning back. The one who delivered the news returns to the radio. More silence. Then he looks this way again and announces: The *Santa Fe* was captured and strafed near South Georgia. And that's all, no message from the Submarine Forces, no order to indicate how this story is playing out, nothing to do but lower the antenna and dive once more at full speed. The *Santa Fe* strafed, there must be wounded, no doubt they've been taken prisoner, our comrades, prisoners, maybe someone's dead; then I think of Mancuso and the dream I had about him, the boat tips as we descend. The *Santa Fe's* out of circulation, someone behind me remarks, and the *Santiago del Estero* was in such bad shape that it probably never even left port. I return to Mancuso, I can't get Mancuso out of my head, I go back to the bullet in Mancuso's body, the last breath escaping from Mancuso's body. Where are you now, old buddy? We're alone, says one of the others, we're alone down here, and he touches his shirt at chest level, right on the pocket where we all know he carries the photo of his mother. Almaraz opens his black leather notebook and tries to write something, leaning against the control room map table. Farther along, in one of the upper bunks, the cook looks at his wristwatch, closes the comic book he's been reading, *Tony* this time, he places it under the pillow, climbs down, and sets out for the galley.

Finally a message today from the Submarine Force, but no one feels calmer. Make our presence known in the Malvinas area, and so in a little while, around midnight, we'll start moving toward the islands. That means we'll have to cross the exclusion zone set by the English. Several of us go to bed with our clothes on; we have to be ready in case they call us to our battle stations. From this point on water and electricity are severely restricted. I climb up to my bunk, fully dressed too; for days now I've been going to bed in my clothes. I arrange the pillow and once more think about Mancuso's death, if that thing about Mancuso's death was really a dream. If it wasn't a dream—and I'm more and more convinced it wasn't—if that wasn't a dream, it's likely that the others weren't either, that somewhere down the line there'll be a tiger waiting for Grunwald, a cadet who hears voices through the walls of the Navy Petty-Officers School of Mechanics, a taxi that Polski will drive through the streets of Mar del Plata, a grave with my name on it. Suddenly everything in here turns red: the night navigation light has just been turned on, and that gives the boat a ghostly appearance. I close my eyes to make everything go black, an opaque surface where I can project those images I thought I'd dreamed.

I'm sitting at the aft table with a book I found somewhere, old, yellowing, missing a cover, who knows how it made its way onto the boat, but you've got to do something while you wait, especially when you're not on duty, so I read the story of a creature that's just finished building his den deep in the earth; next to me, Almaraz writes in his black-covered notebook, from here I can make out a few phrases: We leave today at 0:00 hours, soon we'll enter the two-hundred mile zone that's under English control. Opposite me, on the other side of the table, Nobrega is drawing on legal-size paper with a very soft black pencil, retouching the shading on the figure of a beautiful, curvy woman; many of the others are sleeping; Grunwald, on

the bench next to the torpedo launchers, is working with pliers
and a piece of steel wire; Heredia is cutting strips from a burlap
bag that just a few days ago held potatoes, but they're gone
now, all we eat now are dried foods that need to be rehydrated;
my animal, the animal in my book, runs through the tangled
tunnels of his lair and reaches the center, the storeroom for
provisions, but he can't keep still and he destroys walls and
builds new tunnels. The computer is still broken, Almaraz
notes, as he stares at the torpedo launchers, with the pencil
suspended between his fingers and resting against his mouth.
Nobrega prints in capital block letters in the empty space on the
page above the woman's head: I'M WAITING FOR YOU; Grunwald
maneuvers the pliers and turns the obedient wire into a small
circle with a stub on one side and the rest of the wire, still
unbent, at the other; Heredia has grabbed a monkey wrench
and is wrapping the handle with one of the burlap strips he's
just cut. I go back to my book; the animal rubs his forehead
against the dirt wall of the enclosure to smooth and harden
the structure till his skin bleeds: the damn animal seems
crazy. Radio Colonia talks about an English attack on the
Malvinas any moment now, writes Almaraz in his notebook,
and once more he raises his head and gazes at the torpedo
launchers. DON'T MAKE NOISE WHEN YOU'RE AT SEA, Nobrega
has written on the poster of the woman, this time on the right
side of the sheet, which was empty, and now he goes over and
over each letter, darkening them with his pencil. Grunwald
puts the finishing touches on his wire construction, a pair of
eyeglasses that look like John Lennon's, and he tries them on;
his pale blue eyes shine, sparkle: So? What do you think? he
asks; Almaraz stares at him, smiles, You're a real wacko, he
replies. Soria shows up inside his life jacket, holding a pitcher

of steaming coffee, which he deposits on the table just as Nobrega adds to the poster: YOU DECIDE, beneath the woman's bare feet; Heredia leaves the wrench with the wrapped handle in a tool box on his right and takes another wrench from a box on his left, then he picks up another burlap strip and begins to roll it around the naked handle of the naked tool; Grunwald struts around in his little wire glasses, making exaggerated gestures. Soria watches him and smiles, it's the first time I've seen Soria smile since we weighed anchor; Almaraz jots down something else in his notebook, and I return to the animal who is piling up the pieces he's hunted in the central part of his den and gloating over the smell of the pile of meat; Nobrega draws something on another sheet of legal paper, at first it looks like a skull. Almaraz closes the notebook and tucks it away, along with the pencil, in one of the top pockets of his blue shirt; Soria has walked over to Grunwald, who puts the wire glasses on his nose, and pats him on the back; you look like a bookworm, he says, laughing; my animal runs back and forth, digs, carries, sighs, yawns, stumbles; Nobrega's sketch, which he now retouches and shades in, looks like the outline of a skull; Almaraz gets up from the table and heads for the galley; Heredia keeps plugging away at his task of wrapping tool handles; Cuéllar comes over to the table with another pitcher of coffee; he stands there watching the scene between Grunwald and Soria with those useless glasses; Nobrega writes I'M WAITING FOR YOU on the sketch; I close my book and watch him; MAKE NOISE WHEN YOU'RE AT SEA, he's added. Why are you doing that, man? Cuéllar asks Heredia, who keeps on rolling ragged strips around the tools; to muffle the noise when we use them, and especially if they capture us. *Che*, Bighead, c'mon Cuéllar, Nobrega interrupts, would you put that drawing over there in the control room for me? The one of the woman? Cuéllar asks; yeah, the one of the woman, replies Nobrega as he darkens the letters on the second poster. No, says Grunwald, moving toward the table, send the guys in the control room the one with the skull, and leave us the one with the woman. Okay, says Nobrega, put it over there near the torpedo control panel, then *shhh*, goes someone from the control room; everybody falls silent. My animal tries to decide whether or not he should leave the den; I close the book, leaving the creature alone while he makes up his mind, and I set out for my bunk; I'll either read for a while or I'll fall asleep. As I climb up, I feel my feet all damp and cold, their usual condition ever since I've been here.

The co has ordered us to find out where the noise is coming from, the noise whose signature—as we submariners say—will make us identifiable. Today, since there must be rough seas, judging from how we're moving, you can hear it all the time, so several guys are running from one end of the boat to the other with their heads tilted up to try to detect from inside more or less where the noise is being produced, most likely in the free circulation zone between the deck and the resistant hull. Everyone is quiet, in order to hear better, but it's not easy, there are echoes, rumbles, and the possibility of being discovered at any moment. Then the co decides to send out two men, and I see Olivero putting on his orange waterproof overalls and I wonder, why risk a torpedoman, why send the man who knows the torpedo launchers and the torpedoes better than he knows himself, but down here logic must be different from common sense, or maybe they're sending him because he's small and skinny, or because he volunteered for the mission, I don't know. Now I see Rabellini coming over, the officer in charge of the deck and armaments, also dressed in orange, apparently they're both going to go because they're both underneath the ladder that goes up to the sail. They've been given ten minutes to access the deck, investigate what the hell is causing the noise, and solve it; the sub will surface, the two men have to come out through the escape hatch that's in the exhaust canopy in the conning tower. I see Olivero with his safety harness and the rope with a hook to secure himself, in case he has time for that, a couple of tools wedged into the loops of his harness, the coarse leather gloves, also orange, in both hands. They begin the maneuvers to reach the surface; since it's not my shift I'm not in the engine room; I decide to hang around nearby, just in case, I tell myself; everything here is in case, anyway. A flash of light suddenly takes us by surprise, Olivero, who's on a rung of the ladder, Rabellini, who's still down here and hasn't put on his gloves yet, and me, standing a few steps behind him; somebody takes our picture, or else they take a picture of the moment. I'm sure I'm not in it because, seen from the photographer's perspective, Rabellini is hiding me; I'm like the dark side of the moon. Olivero climbs, somebody clicks the camera again, and I figure this one is of Rabellini alone, who—now I notice his boots wrapped in two black plastic bags—is holding the ladder tight and looking up, but not climbing yet; I'm still on the dark side, and maybe Mainieri—who's moved a couple of steps forward on my right—will show up in the background with that worried expression I can see in profile, but in the photo it'll be seen from the front. Imagine: surfacing and keeping planes and radar from detecting the submarine and the men. Trying to keep them from being seen and dressing them in orange! I'm getting nervous. Rabellini hasn't gone up yet; beside me, the Executive Officer has put on his life jacket and as he pours himself a whisky he tells Gutiérrez not to take his eyes off the Magnavox; someone turns to Rabellini and tells him something I can't quite hear, he takes his hands off the ladder and moves aside a little, then I take advantage of the opportunity to slip away, just as I am, in my dark overalls, and I start climbing up the tube in the conning tower: up there Olivero, who has just reached the upper hatch and is opening it, is outlined, orange against black. Then, through the hole at the end of the tube, a dense blue sky appears, announcing the night and one of those fierce storms that will soon be here; sea water pours in at brief intervals and falls on Olivero in buckets, and then, less heavily, on me. Now Olivero gets out through the side of the conn, most likely he's clutching the iron handrail because the deck has become awfully slippery after several days of submersion. From there he'll probably try to observe, to get his bearings so he can find whatever is causing the noise. He probably looks small and fragile in the light that the day and the storm grudgingly dole out to him, whipped by the constant, dangerous movement of the sea, and paralyzed by the biting cold, in an outfit that's not designed for that cold. Like me, he probably has the strange feeling that nothing exists now, nothing but the endless, gloomy sea that beats furiously against the sub's sail, against us, nothing and no one, only the two of us and something that was making a noise somewhere but which can't be heard anymore because all that greater noise has swallowed it up. I don't know how much time has passed if, in fact, time has passed at all, if it's passing now, but I'm sure I haven't stopped climbing, I climb to the next-to-last rung, and just when I'm about to reach

Olivero, I see him let go of the handrail and struggle into the free circulation zone, and I see—to be honest I only half-see and guess the rest—that Olivero is kneeling on a metal sheet, he's taken off his gloves and is busy unscrewing the long, thick, stubborn screws that hold the metal sheet in place. A sharp jolt throws me off balance and I can't get to him; I yell out that I'm coming to help him, but he's still concentrating on his task, besides, even though we're so close, it's impossible for him to hear me or see me in these dark overalls and this near-total darkness. Another jolt, I grab on tightly to keep from falling— the sub keeps moving, if it stopped, the violent rocking would be even worse —and behind the water gushing in, enclosed in a small space where he barely fits, I think I see Olivero lift up the black metal sheet, stick in his hand and remove something, something I can't make out but suspect he's caught, because of the shape one of his hands seems to be taking now as it crawls up his waterproof overalls in search of a pocket where he can deposit his prey. Now he tries to replace the metal sheet he just removed a few moments ago. I can't do anything to help him from here, because the two of us won't fit in that space, but I stick around anyway, maybe I can say something so he'll know we haven't left him alone. Olivero knows—we both know— that if the radar operator gets a signal, the hatch will close and the boat will start to dive, leaving him outside, forever floating, a ridiculous orange fallen from a tree into the water. If that should happen, I decide, I'll stay behind too, it's terrible to die alone, though maybe it's not all that bad to die in the sea; I would rather die in the sea if I could choose, and I think I remember hearing Olivero once say that—or something like that. It's nighttime now, you can't see a thing, barely a shape that he'll no doubt try to put back in place, groping to insert those long screws into the holes at either end of the metal sheet, screws that we all know will never fit back in again. I cross my fingers and think I can see—or imagine I see—in the thick darkness my eyes are adjusting to, Olivero's smile, as if he's seen me in spite of the darkness, as if he knew that, in the depths of this darkness, I'm here.

I think someone is yelling from below that we've run out of time, that we're being tracked by radar, but I don't know— with all this noise—if it's true or if I've imagined it; regardless, I stand still and wait. Now I hear Olivero come out; extending my hand, I grope my way till I manage to grab his arm and squeeze it for a second; there's not much time left, and we begin our descent right now; he responds by grabbing mine for a moment, a greeting between two blind men, an act of recognition between two ghosts; and so I understand that I should go down first and start descending, while he closes the upper hatch; without saying a word to one another each of us imitates the other's movements, skipping rungs. Close to the bottom I fall and roll astern, leaving room for Olivero; now I hear him fall in the same place where I had been a fraction of a second earlier. Someone above us closes the second hatch and announces: we're diving, they're looking for us. Olivero reaches into his raincoat pocket and takes out a pair of soldering pliers that someone left behind on a repair job, shows it to Grunwald, who has come dashing over, helpfully, from the torpedo launcher. Olivero is white, a yellowish white that gleams against the orange of his raincoat; sitting on the floor, he smiles with his purple lips, waving the pliers in his right hand. I stand, dripping, my overalls are dripping, my socks are dripping, a pool of water is forming around me.

Grunwald clutches the pliers, shows them to the rest of the guys who have come over, curious to see what was causing the noise; he makes exaggerated gestures with his hands, like he usually does when he talks, his hands intact, each one with its five fingers. The electronic equipment goes off to indicate approaching aircraft. Olivero stands and starts walking toward his station by the torpedoes. Those remaining head for their battle stations. And so do I.

We keep traveling toward the patrol area we've been assigned. Today we're not listening to the radio, so we don't know anything about what's happening outside. We go about our daily routine, nothing new, it's an empty day. Empty like the day of the chest pain that knocked me to the floor of the engine room and all the ones that followed until the moment when the noise woke me up. Days I can't quite recall, which disappeared from my memory as if a worm had eaten them, like the house borer that attacked the tie beams in the little chalet. It was about waking up in the middle of the night and hearing the sound of the house borer, a unique, recognizable sound, it was turning on the light, staring up at the portion of wooden roof I could see and not finding anything. The house borer works from the inside, the beetle eats greedily, patiently, until the wood weakens, hardly more than sawdust, and breaks. Sometimes I would wake up all sweaty, with a strong pressure in my chest, convinced that the roof had fallen down on us. During the day we didn't hear it; the noises of activity during the daylight hours tend to cover it up completely. When I was on campaign, days submerged in the sea, I had the feeling that all of it was just a distant nightmare, a nasty trick played by my imagination. But it was a question of putting my feet back on the ground, going back home, and, once night fell, hearing it again. Everyone seemed to have solutions to offer, some of them obviously ridiculous, others impossible. In the end we found a company that guaranteed its elimination. And then, when they finished the job and made sure the extermination was thorough and we thought we were going to finally get some peace, we became even more alert to it than before; I remember how Mama suddenly turned down the volume on the radio: Just a minute, let me listen, she would say to us, and we'd all wait quietly—María, my mother, and I—to see if we could hear the house borer. I also remember sitting around chatting and suddenly falling silent, in the middle of dinner, not saying a word to one another, each of us looking up slyly, out of the corners of our eyes, as if focusing on some spot on the ceiling would help us hear better, and then taking up the discussion again if nothing had happened, as if it had just been a natural pause in a family's dinner conversation. Once I came home from the base and found Mama sitting at the kitchen table with Doña Aurelia, a *mate* in her hand, both of them silently looking at the ceiling. Sometimes we thought the noise had gone away, and with it the house borer, because we never did see that house borer, we heard it: the noise was the beetle. Other times, I woke up again in the middle of the night, convinced I had heard it; I'd turn on the light like before, like always, and I couldn't tell if I was really hearing it or only thought I did, the illusion of sound, like an echo lodged in my memory. Maybe it never left; it hung around quietly for a while to confuse us and came back later, not for the tie beams in the little chalet, but to swallow up those days of my life that I can't get back again and try to reassemble hypothetically, to keep everything from collapsing on me suddenly—life, you know?—as if it was the roof of the chalet, and to keep it from squashing me altogether. Then I imagine that one of the boys who worked with me in those days trying to fix the engine we could never manage to jump-start, Albaredo maybe, cried out, yelling that I was on the destroyed floor, unconscious, and a few of them together pulled me out through the forward hatch and the ambulance came and took me to the Naval Hospital, and meanwhile someone called the neighbor lady because at our house—even though we've been asking for years—they still haven't put in a phone, to notify María, taking care not to frighten Mama, and I was there for one day, connected to monitors, with medication and some tests, and they must have told them later that it was nothing serious, that it had just been a scare, that maybe I should watch what I ate, that I should use less salt and stuff like that, and that I should rest a little and then just go back to work, to the sub and the engines, since that's my thing, after all. And I must have used those days to rest and recover, to finish reading that book I left off at the war scene, the one with the horse whose back was raw, which left such an impression on me. That's what happened to me, I repeat it in my head over and over again, with some variations, but more or less the same, so often that I don't know anymore if I made it up or if it really took place, like what happened to us with the house borer, which we don't know if it was or wasn't there. Anyway, that's starting to happen to me with other things, too; today I tried to remember Javier's birthday, my cousin who's like a brother to me, and I couldn't, or that way María has of drying her hands on her apron when she's finished washing the dishes, and I always used to be able to see her as if she was right in front of me and now I can only capture it in a couple of vague words that don't mean anything: what is "that way" if you can't add a moving image to whatever it is you're saying, the details of the moment itself, what it awakens in you? It's as if my memory is filling up with holes, like the stinking, wounded back of that horse in the book, as if the house borer was inside me, devouring my memories, slowly but constantly, leaving me empty, a pure present that sooner or later will also be devoured.

Today, as expected, we arrived at our patrol area and stayed there all day long. I'm tired of sleeping. My sleep has changed, I've gotten used to sleeping in the afternoon, and at night I'm wide awake. Since we can't be up when it's not our shift but need to stay lying down instead so we won't get tired and also to save oxygen, we don't know what to do in bed anymore. Now I'm in my bunk: from here I can see Olivero, he's on his stomach, half propped up, the weight of his body resting on his forearms, a notebook on the bed quilt, and he's writing, writing, sometimes he stops to think a little, slowly adding one word or another and then he picks up speed and writes, writes, writes. Could it be a letter? Could it be stories for a personal journal? Some of the others say he writes poems for those girlfriends of his. Now he's picked up the notebook, turned over on his back, and is reading what he wrote. I take out the book I'd left under my pillow and start reading, too: the animal couldn't handle being outside his den and ended up returning to his blind, enclosed world. Olivero climbs down from his bunk, takes a few steps aft and goes into the galley. The animal in the book now suspects he's being stalked, he's scared and listens constantly for the sound of something approaching but which can't be seen from the lair. Olivero returns from the galley with a couple of small bottles that he deposits in his bunk while standing in the passageway; he carefully tears some pages out of his notebook, they've been written on, most likely the ones he's just finished writing; he places one sheet on top of another, rolls them up, unscrews the top of one of the little bottles, sticks the pages in the bottle, replaces the top. He stands there for a few seconds and looks at the two bottles resting on his bed, then goes to his locker and stores them there. Till gradually, says my animal, sobriety takes over as I wake up altogether. I can hardly understand what the hurry is, I take a deep breath and inhale the peace that reigns in my house and which I have disturbed, I return to the place where I rest, and fall asleep immediately, overcome by exhaustion. Olivero has gone back to his bunk, he's stretched out there; now he closes the little black curtain, most likely he's getting ready to sleep.

The others are in bed, each one in his bunk, calm, quiet, eyes closed, trying to sleep. I'm in my bunk, too, but I still can't fall asleep, I'm staring upward, the bottom of the bunk above me is like a ceiling, or a cover, for mine; I look up and see that bunk, knowing that mine is beneath it and underneath mine, in turn, there's another, with someone who's also sleeping or trying to sleep; we're all piled up, maybe all of us are dead, one coffin on top of another, only we don't realize it yet. Is it possible for someone to die and not know it?

I wake up startled; I've had nightmares again, some dreams are repeated. They're more or less the same, with small variations. There's activity in the sonar area, something's going on. I head for the galley to get a coffee; Almaraz is pouring himself a cup from one of the little steel pitchers, and just as the coffee reaches the middle of the cup, they call us to our battle stations. I forget about the coffee. Almaraz takes a gulp from his cup, leaves it in the sink, and starts out toward the control compartment; he's handling the stern planer in combat. I head for the engine room and on the way I see the three sonar operators working: Elizalde and Medrano seated, with their earphones on; Cuéllar, standing, takes the earphones from Medrano to confirm a sound and then returns them to him. They're really not there in the sonar, they're not here, they're outside, in the water, all ears, penetrating the depths of a labyrinth of echoes and sounds, waiting for whatever the sea will bring them. Hydrophonic sound detected at azimuth zero seven nine, says Cuéllar after consulting Elizalde and Medrano, and they begin plotting for classification of the target. Direction zero seven zero, turn forty degrees to port, the co orders, and we set course for the enemy ship, following the sonar operators' estimates. Albaredo, Soria, and Torres are in the engine room; the crew for this shift is complete yet again, I don't understand why the hell there's someone extra every time, probably someone got confused when they were setting up the shifts. In any case I take a walk around to check the engines, even though I'm sure Albaredo's done it already, I need to be busy, like everyone else, during the wait, this time of "we'll see what happens." Just then I discover that my boots are no longer where I left them, that prank again, no doubt they took them to the usual place, but now that's the least of our worries: we're definitely at war, the enemy is approaching, and who knows how the hell this will all turn out. And so I stick around here in case they need me, but looking out a little toward the rudder area, and with my ear alert to what the sonar operator might be saying so as to detect the tiniest gesture. They must be listening to the beating of the ship's motor blades and trying to detect … Destroyer, type twenty-one or twenty-two, Medrano suddenly whispers toward the control room. A sonar emission, type one eight four, he adds. And everything grows silent and slow, only gestures, movements synched to the rhythm of our waiting. The co orders us to turn in the direction of the target—Almaraz and Polski operate the diving planes; Navarrete, the rudder— and to increase speed to the maximum in order to shorten the distance, engines going full blast and in the control room there's a lot of activity. The co orders the combat periscope up; an officer stands next to him; now he prepares to look outside, trying to sight the target. There's a lot of fog, the co says to the officer, and while the officer, in turn, looks through the periscope, I tell myself that maybe it's that same fog that hid our departure from the port, the same one that's always surrounded us and sails with us like just another silent crew member. Down periscope, orders the co; the officer wasn't able to see anything, either, nothing beside the fog. The target is operating with choppers, Elizalde announces toward the control room, at a speed of eighteen knots, he adds. Now, even though nobody says anything, we all know that it's going to be a tricky business; it won't be easy to fire a torpedo and then flee from the choppers. I walk slowly forward. Rocha comes out of the head and walks toward his post. Egea crosses my path with a tray holding two empty glasses and walks into the galley; I keep on going, the cook is lying in his bunk, reading a *Nippur of Lagash* comic book; farther along, on the table opposite the torpedoes, a pencil wobbles, swaying lightly, nervously back and forth, unable to decide if it should roll toward one side or the other. From the bow I see Olivero leaning against one of the torpedo launcher tubes. Grunwald and Heredia sit on the bench on the port side, their profiles toward the torpedoes; I stop a few steps away from them. The co's order to fire a torpedo at the detected target reaches us. It will be a manual launch because the fire control computer still doesn't work. The sub's engines are shut down in order to be able to operate and do the calculations more precisely. An officer appears with the necessary data: Olivero starts the maneuvers, opens the valve to flood the tube; you can hear the torpedo propellers start up with a dull hiss; the launching hatch opens. Behind me the others carefully begin to disassemble the bunks and pile them up at starboard so as to leave access open to the torpedo room. Grunwald looks at Heredia: we have to give it a name, he says; it's the first real torpedo launched by the Argentine Navy. A name? Heredia asks. Yeah, for the torpedo—*Mar del Plata*, let's call it *Mar del Plata*, and let's cross our fingers for it to hit the target. No doubt Marini has just pushed the launch button on the computer (which actually works, the launch command, but not the firing calculations), because I hear the rotor blades speed up and the torpedo shoots off, it tips a little as it enters the sea, remains suspended in the water for a fraction of a second, and then speeds toward the target, connected to the boat by a thread, an umbilical cord that feeds it with data so it can find its objective, unwinding to let it advance. We wait in anticipation, the others behind me have stopped, each in the middle of what he was doing, at the exact moment the torpedo took off, speechless, staring toward Olivero, toward the tube, now empty of the torpedo and full of water. It cut the thread, Olivero whispers, and now we all know that it will be guided by its acoustic head searching for a noise to attack. And then I imagine what it might be like, that thing we'll never see from this enclosed, blind ship, the torpedo explosion against the enemy boat, the fire, the smoke, the shock, the wounds, the blood, things we sometimes see in movies but which now can happen in reality, though how can we know it, we won't see anything, we'll just sense the echo of the blast and maybe feel a kind of jolt, but not the screams, the screams of pain and fear, the noise of death silenced by the water, the others—those outside– floating by. But the detonation doesn't happen, minutes go by and nothing, maybe the torpedo kept on going, maybe its battery ran out and it sank to the bottom of the sea, deactivated, dead. Then I see Grunwald elbowing Heredia and pointing upward, tracing circles in the air with his raised index finger: I can hear them too, chopper rotors, the convoy of choppers that escort the boat we're trying to hit have detected the wake of our torpedo from the air and are looking for us. Just then Grunwald closes his eyes, opens them with a start, and says to Heredia: Hey, buddy, your wife had the baby, a boy, look at the time, you'll see exactly when he was born. Heredia checks his watch and hugs him. Evasive maneuvers begin. We dive. The others go back to their work of dismantling the bunks; soon they'll have to load another torpedo. I decide to return to the engine room. The boat lists, the curtain behind the aft table falls open a little and I can see my boots. We're diving deeper and deeper, you can hear the rotors of the choppers, a little muffled, but we know they're still there.

Torpedo splashdown in the water, says Elizalde, and even though his voice is gentle I leap up as if I'd heard a scream. With the bunks dismantled, we sleep right on the floor, on top of whatever blankets or clothing each one can find and pile up in any available corner. Maximum depth, the co orders, and evasive maneuvers begin. Fernández is ordered to eject an Alka-Seltzer to produce bubbles and disorient the torpedo, so he runs to the petty officers' head, where the ejector is kept, but the door is closed, there's someone inside; he bangs on the door desperately, some people whisper at him not to make noise, the torpedo searches out the noise, searches us out as if sniffing the sound, any tiny thing it might detect. Heredia steps out of the head buck naked, pulling on his underwear, his overalls down around his ankles; Fernández goes inside and starts maneuvers: he opens the ejector compartment, inserts the decoy into the tube, now he has to open the valve to fill the tube with water, but he decides to skip that step in order to save a few seconds; then he goes to open the air valve above the toilet so that the pressurized air injected in the ejector tube will propel the fake target, but he can't, he applies pressure, tries with both hands, but the valve is stuck and doesn't move a millimeter. Nobrega, who's watching him, makes a sign toward the bow and also pops into the bathroom to help; Grunwald comes from the bow with a crowbar, uses it as a lever, and manages to open the valve. The decoy shoots out and starts to bubble; Heredia finishes pulling up his overalls, crosses himself, heads for the torpedo area; a mouthful of water enters through the ejector, which all the guys remaining in the head try to seal off; the three of them gush water as they listen to the enemy torpedo approach—its humming rotor spinning wildly—with greater and greater force; Linares clutches the rosary that dangles from his neck and moves his lips silently, he must be praying as the torpedo comes closer, closer, and I say to myself that maybe in the ship that fired it there's someone imagining our explosion, the terrible hole in the sub's armor that will increase pressure till it smashes us to bits, from the inside to the outside, each and every one of us, as if it's inflating us and inflating us till it makes us burst. There won't be time for anything, not even to scream or run away or hear or see, the blood will tint the water a crackling red that will be diluted little by little till it turns back into plain water. The lights flicker, our batteries are running low, the CO asks: Battery remaining? Twenty percent, they reply. The torpedo whizzes by to starboard. Remaining? Fifteen percent, and the torpedo continues on course, I hear it, it whizzes and keeps going, whizzes and keeps going. Remaining? Ten percent, the sub vibrates, the CO orders us to turn off the machines to conserve the batteries, an even greater silence falls, there's no sound at all, we float gently and the transparent water goes back to red again, and the blood returns to our limbs and our limbs to our bodies and our bodies to the sub and the hole seals up and the metal plate is restored while the torpedo continues on course till we can't hear its fucking little rotor blade anymore.

A crash, as if a giant piece of glass has broken, startles us. Depth charge at port, whispers Elizalde, and so the maneuvers to avoid the enemy begin again, an enemy we can hear but never see. A new depth charge shakes us even harder, we dive quickly, everything tilts, a jar of something rolls past my feet, I follow it with my eyes. Another depth charge, this time near the bow, jolts us; that's three, says Heredia, nervously scratching his head; the jar has stopped by Grunwald's feet, which are wrapped in several pairs of socks; Green peas? Grunwald asks Heredia, whose only reply is a shrug. We turn to port and another charge shakes us, though less violent this time; I look up toward the pipes, there's a small leak, one of the other guys shows up with pliers, one of those pliers whose handles Heredia had covered so patiently; some people have started putting on their life jackets even though the CO hasn't given the order; then comes the wallop of another explosion as we dive even deeper, now the jar goes rolling from Grunwald toward me; four more explosions, Heredia continues to count, the jar stops next to my feet, which are wrapped in several pairs of blue socks, one on top of another. Capers, the label says, they're capers. Grunwald looks at Heredia: Relax, he says, it'll pass. Another depth charge whips us, and another right after that one, each one feels like you have a metal helmet on your head and somebody's hammering on it. Just relax, we'll come out of this and go home, Grunwald says to Heredia, and How do you …? but Heredia's question is swallowed up by the noise of a new explosion and now there are no more questions or answers; no one's talking anymore. Another charge stuns and shakes us, that's eight so far, Heredia tallies. We dive even deeper, trying to dodge them, fucking choppers; nine anti-submarine charges, but this time no one says anything, not even Heredia; others imitate the first guys and put on their life jackets; now the jar rolls down to Heredia's feet, as he watches its gentle rocking, like tremors; Capers, capers, he starts to read aloud, what's this for? No idea, Grunwald replies; another new charge stuns us and shakes us, and why the life jacket, I wonder, if at this depth and with this pressure no one will be able to survive. Another charge, now the jar rolls past my feet and then, together with the new quake, a noise startles me, it startles the others, too: it scrapes the metal plate of the boat, it creaks as if it's about to split open against the rocky ocean floor. Grunwald jumps out of his

143

chair, a few of the others run toward the bow to add weight to the boat. Olivero desperately struggles to fill the tanks with ballast; most likely the navigation chart got messed up and we're touching bottom, so Olivero—and now Grunwald—work to keep us from ricocheting and having the rotor blade break on us, keeping us trapped here on the bottom forever, those with life jackets and those without, all of us, the same, smashed to pieces. Another explosive charge falls, but this time it doesn't seem so close; the jar shakes but doesn't move. The CO orders all machinery stopped; the sub, heavy now, floats gently; everyone is silent and still, grabbing on to whatever they can to keep from falling while the boat carves a cradle in the ocean floor, which seems sandy now; it rocks a little, finds its place. The jar moves, I follow it with my eyes and see Soria rushing into the head, the door doesn't shut: here at the bottom the boat compresses and now the door to the head, which was open when we started to dive, doesn't fit in its frame anymore and won't close all the way; another charge explodes but we barely move. The other guys' faces look white, transparent, damp, we turn paler and paler, all of us, the others and, no doubt, me too, sort of moldy for lack of natural light, from so much breathing condensed in here. Another charge; it feels like they're sweeping the area, most likely behind the choppers there are destroyers or aircraft carriers. And then another, this one jerks us with greater force, it feels like my head's about to explode, the jar hasn't come back, it's stuck against a blanket that's lying on the floor, all rolled up. The others look ridiculous with those life jackets that couldn't save them anyway; the CO, however, hasn't put his on; neither has Grunwald, but he *has* put on his wire-framed glasses and is making faces at Heredia to crack him up; Torres rummages in his locker till he finds and removes the three cassettes he's recorded for his girlfriend and puts them in a little plastic bag which he ties to his life preserver. Now we're quiet down below, I feel kind of weak and decide to move around a little; I take a few steps aft, there's another guy stashing a small white towel and a little axe in his plastic bag; I want to see how things are going in the engine room so I head in that direction; Nobrega stows a towel and a deodorant in a plastic bag and ties it to his waist; another charge shakes us, I think my head's going to explode, I hold it between my hands, not moving, and suddenly I have a vision of the scene with the horse from that book I was reading, but I still don't know if I finished it after I was hospitalized (if, in fact, I was). I forget certain things I'd like to remember and I remember the ones I'd like to forget; they come to me now at awkward times without my calling them, they barge in and force me to deal with them: the horse smells rotten, like corpses, like a dead man, but he's alive and on his feet, tied to the post so he won't run away, so he won't lie down on the ground to wait for death; tied and standing, he waits, not knowing what for, but he waits, his back raw, the only living thing in the middle of so much death, alive, stinking, and filled with pus, with streams of pus dripping down his flanks. I don't want to see the horse, I don't want to smell him, I don't want to, but I see him and I smell him and my stomach turns over and I rush toward the head, not making any noise, sick to my stomach and light-headed, but the damn toilet I'm supposed to use is occupied and I bang on the door with my closed fist, the door that doesn't close, while at the same time I feel something liquid and acid rising from my stomach to my mouth, and in a desperate attempt to keep from vomiting and spilling it all out, I swallow it, I swallow it together with the disgusting, disturbing memory of that war horse I once read about, I swallow it together with this endless, uncertain wait. I give up waiting to use the head, it won't be necessary now; I also give up on the idea of going to the engine room, I turn on my heels and return to the bow; the sub shakes once more, the jar of capers rolls past my feet again, thirty-four, Heredia says, that makes thirty-four, and it looks like I'll never meet my son, he adds. We'll go home, Grunwald tells him, the woman who does cures with dogs told me so. Who? Heredia asks. A woman from Tres Arroyos who does cures with dogs, she told me I'd get back home safely; But she told you, not me; you, too, you'll … A new charge. That makes thirty-five, Heredia counts, will they ever stop? I feel uneasy, though better, and I'd rather move, I set off again toward the engine room; on the way I see someone stowing a toothbrush and a small tube of toothpaste in his plastic bag, he rolls it all up and sticks it inside his life jacket; I cross paths with the CO, who's heading from the control room to somewhere behind me. The open door of the officers' cabin allows me to see the Executive Officer stashing cigarettes in a plastic bag, and the Hyena's smile appears before my eyes again. I continue on my way; when I reach the control room I see that Polski is sitting on the stool at the map table, the lamplight turned on very low, he bends over a little, carefully studying the maps, he follows some lines with one finger, jots something down on a blank sheet of paper, looks again, traces his finger along the paper once more, jots some-thing down again; I watch him out of sheer curiosity. The CO returns from his regular route from the control room to his cabin and back again; this time he walks up to the chart table, stops behind Polski, observes him, What are you doing, Polski? he

146

asks; I'm marking the locations of the ranches closest to the coast, sir, and the distances we'd have to walk in case we need to disembark. The CO looks him right in the eye as he zips his jacket up to his neck; Take it easy, Polski, nobody's going to get out of here, he replies and continues on his way, from the control room to his cabin, and then, no doubt, from his cabin to the control room. Polski folds the sheet of paper again and again until it's just a tiny, compact rectangle which he tosses into the basket secured underneath the table, turns off the lamp, and returns to his post. It's been a while now, a moment—how can you tell how long it's been when time behaves so randomly around here—since we've been jolted by a depth charge; it seems they've given us up for lost. I keep on walking; in front of the sonar equipment, Elizalde is stuffing packs of cigarettes into a little bag; I continue on to the engine room. Albaredo, Soria, and Torres are there, standing next to one another, calmly, looking down. Then the ping of enemy sonar echoes in our ears like a sharp twinge, it repeats, penetrating from one end of the boat to the other, it stalks us and studies us. Those on the outside are looking for us. We stay here, on the inside, our only possible place, waiting. The only damn thing we can do is wait.

Someone says it's 8 PM already, though here it's always night-time, or daytime, or some uncertain thing that's not night or day, just the artificial light of the fluorescent bulbs in this enclosed tube. The CO has ordered us to lift off from the bottom; everyone who's on duty goes to their stations. In the forward section, someone puts back all those uncomfortable life jackets that most of the guys have taken off. I've found my book again, in the middle of the mess that was left behind when the bunks were taken down, the book about the animal in his labyrinth, so I sit on the floor, on top of a little pile of clothes, near one of the lights that are always on, and I start to read. Those who aren't at their stations are still curled up in some cleared spot on the ground, trying to sleep. Now they turn off the engines and we float, carried along by a current that leads us toward the patrol area assigned to us around the islands. We're positioned to snorkel and change air. In the torpedo area, Grunwald helps Heredia wrap the handles of other tools. Suddenly the air circulation noise stops and we all know that happens when the sonarman needs more silence so he can identify a noise: down here, listening is like seeing. There's a piercing silence; an officer whispers the order to cover our combat posts, an order that circulates from man to man; before me I see feet stuffed into socks or sneakers; someone remarks that the noises might indicate a group of boats that seem to be returning from Puerto Argentino. Could they have bombed anything? Grunwald asks softly, but the question remains floating until it dissolves into the thick air surrounding us because there's no time for answers, or there's no energy for those answers we don't want to hear. We submerge again, to hide on the bottom once more, till they pass over us; we can't shoot off torpedoes here, so we remain quiet and still, or there won't be enough air. The buzz of circulating air returns, the lights are turned off, leaving only the most essential ones: I can't read anymore. Might as well try to sleep a little. Almaraz informs the Executive Officer that the amount of CO_2 is 1.2 and if it keeps going up we're going to have to control the oxygen supply. Egea comes by with a tray, offering glasses of juice, the only thing there is to drink. The CO decides to authorize Almaraz to start controlling oxygen, we're at the limit of our breathable supply, and of course our nerves and fear don't help; more air gets used up: Will we be doomed to suffocate here, to lose our strength slowly, fall asleep and die, or will we be doomed to explode into pieces because of some torpedo or depth bomb that eventually will find us? But no one dares to ask the question. What's for sure is that there'll be no lit stove or hot food today. The Executive Officer bursts out of his cabin, scratching his head and walking toward the command post: Excuse me, Captain, sir, permission to smoke; the co stands there looking at him as if he can't quite understand, turns his head, looks at Almaraz; then he confronts the inquiring eyes of the Executive Officer, who's already started to pull a pack of cigarettes out of his jacket pocket. Maceda, we're controlling oxygen, he replies dryly; Oh, okay, sorry, he says as he replaces the cigarette in the pack; Go and rest like the other men, the co adds; then Maceda turns on his heels and returns to his bunk. I feel tired, straighten out the clothing and blankets I've settled on top of, feel something compact and hard with my hand and pull aside the blanket: it's the jar of capers. I grab onto it like it's the wood that's going to save me from this shipwreck. I close my eyes.

I'm awakened by Rocha announcing that he has a bad headache and a very dry nose; it seems the others have the same symptoms because the nurse goes around distributing aspirins to everyone who needs them; I don't take anything, I don't feel anything unusual, and if I did have pain I'd rather just put up with it and let it go away by itself. We're going to rise to snorkel level, which is to say we're staying at around sixteen meters below sea level, but with the snorkel outside, to change the air and charge the batteries. Somebody says it's five AM; we've been on the bottom for almost a day. Sometimes I wonder if I'll ever see daylight again. For now these lights are turned on and I'm fine with that, I go back to my book, trying to find the page where I left off. There's activity in the galley. Loza is making a rice stew that we'll all eat while sitting on the floor or leaning against whatever we can find, trying not to make any noise at all. A strong smell of shit invades the atmosphere, which always happens when we snorkel, even more this time, after so many hours of being submerged and without venting. The animal curls up in one of his favorite places in his den, and stays there as if he wants to sleep, but he doesn't want to sleep, he just plans to stay there, calm and still, smelling the scents of the accumulated prey in the central area, but he's overcome by drowsiness and after a while falls sound asleep.

We're still sailing northeast, says someone nearby; it looks like we're heading toward the María zone, the area we've been assigned to patrol. One part of the crew occupies its posts, the rest are now setting up the bunks again, putting them back in their places, creating a little order. While we snorkel they raise the antenna to see if any news of what's going on outside can be reached through Radio Colonia in Uruguay; it's the only way to find out anything in this enclosed cylinder, buried at the bottom of the ocean; apparently Argentine radio stations aren't reliable, as someone suggested a few days ago. We have no news through official channels either. A couple of guys stand around the radio, someone asks for the equipment to be connected to the speaker beside the galley so we can all hear, the co says no, making noise isn't safe, if there's any important news he himself will pass it along to the crew, we don't need rumors and distractions, let everyone go on doing his own job. The area is cleared; the Executive Officer, who is among those huddled around the radio, suddenly stands up, goes over to the CO, and whispers something to him, but I can't quite hear it from where I am; the CO's expression changes, now he looks worried, he shakes his head no, don't communicate anything till it's official, I think I can read his lips, but I'm not really sure he actually said that. I don't know exactly how, I don't understand what he's saying, but it's clear that the second-in-command persists, his gestures looked annoyed, and again a refusal from the CO. The Executive Officer returns to the officers' cabin, goes inside and closes the door. The CO takes up his route again from the command post to his cabin; once he gets there, he turns around to resume the return trip, from his cabin to the command post.

It seems like I've slept for quite a while. I stand up to stretch my legs, which have gone numb. Then an officer spreads the announcement that the CO wants to talk to all crew members who are awake. A group of men quickly forms between the galley and the command post, around eighteen of them, all in suspense. It's just been confirmed that the cruiser *General Belgrano* has been sunk. No one says anything, some make fists at the ends of their dangling arms, others close their eyes, others open their mouths without letting a word escape, others smack their foreheads, while still others rub the backs of their heads vigorously; the CO surveys their expressions with a glance; one of the group, breaking that uncomfortable silence, says that there were four submariners on the cruiser; no one knows yet if there are survivors, the CO adds; the Executive Officer is there, too; he exchanges a look with the CO when

151

the captain orders the men back to their posts. I stay where I am, beside the periscope; the second-in-command addresses the CO; he tells him something in such a quiet voice that I can only make out random phrases: computer ... inefficiency ...helpless ... offensive capacity. The CO lets him talk and then replies with words that disintegrate without reaching me, through air that is now almost solid. The second-in-command turns and walks away. The snorkel operation is over, the batteries are charged, the air has been replenished, and immersion maneuvers begin.

You won't believe this, exclaims someone nearby, startling me awake, the Captain is smoking! I open my eyes and see Egea crossing from the CO's cabin to the galley with a tray that holds the remnants of a meal, some cutlery, an empty glass, and some used paper napkins. I glance toward the stern and see that there are four guys standing next to the radio, all four of them intently scratching their heads, one after another, as if they were following a secret, inexplicable plan; the CO walks from his cabin to the command post with a lit cigarette squeezed between his lips. Rojas says something to Grunwald, who pops out immediately in search of Heredia; he finds him in the kitchen, serving coffee and chatting with Egea, who has emptied the tray and is wiping it down with a damp dishcloth. C'mere, man, Rojas just heard something, some news he wants to give you in person. Heredia leaves the dishcloth on top of the counter and hurries, followed by Grunwald, over to the radio equipment; he walks up to Rojas, who still has earphones on and is listening attentively, and taps him on the shoulder. Rojas holds up his hand, signaling him to wait. Grunwald stops behind Heredia, Soria passes by on the way to the engine room, carrying his tape recorder and cassettes. Rojas takes off his earphones, you're the father of a boy, he says to Heredia; he was born two days ago, May 1. See? I told you, I knew it! Grunwald pats him on the back, while turning to Rojas to ask: Did they tell you what time the kid was born? Around three in the afternoon, Rojas replies, smiling at Heredia. See? Grunwald insists, exactly when I told you! Remember? Three o'clock, when they were firing the depth charges, see? he repeats, as he gives Heredia a hug, and he's gonna be a worker, *che*, because he was born on May Day … or maybe he'll turn out to be a lazy bum! Heredia pulls away from Grunwald a little; his eyes are filled with tears; don't pay any attention to me, he's gonna be a worker and support you, Grunwald tries to joke, don't cry, *che*, you'll meet him soon, you'll see, just stick with me, 'cause I swear I'm going home, *we're* going home. Rojas puts the earphones back on and returns to his job; Heredia and Grunwald walk right past me; I follow them with my eyes and watch them go into the galley, Heredia to find the half-filled cup that he left on the counter; Grunwald to pour himself some coffee. On the other side of the corridor, the co's cabin door is ajar and I can hear someone who isn't the co say that we'll have to return to port to fix the computer. I think I recognize the voice of the Executive Officer adding: even if it's back to Rawson, because like this, with no computer, we're out of commission, we have no way to attack or to defend ourselves. Grunwald and Heredia come out of the galley, laughing: someone— the captain, I imagine—pushes the cabin door from inside, closing it. Of course I'll be the godfather, and you have no idea how I'm gonna spoil him, Grunwald says to Heredia as they walk away toward the bow.

I can't feel my feet; I've just realized I can't feel my feet, I can see them, at the ends of my legs, covered by socks that used to be blue and are now a blackish brown, but I don't feel them. I move them, my head gives the order and I can move them forward, first one, then the other, and then I walk, but I have the sensation of floating, because I can't feel the pressure of my soles against the floor. I try to explain to myself what's happening to me and I tell myself they must have fallen asleep from lying in an uncomfortable position, but I don't have the usual prickly feeling, though walking like this, even if it feels strange, gets me where I want to go. And so I walk, in order to see if I can get back the lost sensation. Gathered around the table at the bow, Soria, Torres, and Albaredo have finished their shift and are eating. It looks like they're rescuing the survivors of the *General Belgrano*, Torres remarks; How do you know? Soria asks; Rojas heard it on the radio; well, anyway, there must have been many dead, Albaredo cuts in, you can't survive too long in icy water, especially if you're wounded. I also found out that there was heavy ground fighting today on the islands, Torres adds. A voice behind me interrupts them: *Che*, Albaredo, Officer Garmendia is calling you; the converter is out of order and we need to activate the auxiliary. I'm coming, Albaredo replies, wiping his mouth with a napkin that he leaves on his enamel dish, he also picks up the utensils, lays them in an X across his plate, collects everything in his right hand, stands and starts walking. I decide to follow him, maybe he'll need me, I can help too. I look at my feet; I still can't feel them, but I give them the order and they start to move; I catch up with Albaredo just as he stops before the galley's open door. He deposits the dish with the utensils and the used napkin in the sink and heads toward the engine room; I bring up the rear. Beside the fact that the fire control computer isn't working, now we have to sail with the emergency converter. We sure are doing great.

Soria has come out of the engine room and is on his way to the galley in search of coffee for everyone. Torres and Albaredo are still cleaning the grease off their hands with solvent and a rag. Everything is done by hand in this kind of boat, all with manpower, human skill. The emergency converter is still working; now we'll have to wait and hope it doesn't get hit or we'll be completely out of commission and exposed. Soria enters the engine room with a pitcher of coffee in one hand and two more in the other. We've sunk the destroyer *Sheffield*, he informs us, and nobody dares say a word in response as the new arrival holds out his arms toward Torres and Albaredo to distribute the coffee. I heard it when the co was telling Ghezzi, Soria explains; they want us to go to the last location where we saw the boat and confirm the sinking. They clink the pitchers in a toast, and since they don't need me, I'd just as soon return to my corner, my book, and my threatened animal. A naval battle, I suddenly remember as I leave the engine room, water, hit, sunk. Everything was clean then, a cross on a piece of paper, something about strategy, a little luck, a little studying the other guy's face, but clean: pencil, a perfect grid traced with the same wooden carpenter's square we used to take to school, boats that were just little squares drawn in pencil or ballpoint or felt-tip pen, and coming from the other side, temporary enemies who later we would play ball with on the same team. Hit, sunk, but no trace of blood, or screaming, or fire, or icy water that cuts off your breath, or fear, or death. The

General Belgrano, hit, sunk. The *Sheffield* hit, sunk. Lieutenant Ghezzi is sitting at the chart table, his elbows resting on the smooth surface of the navigation chart spread out on top of the glass cover; the light from underneath barely brightens his face, his eyes are fixed on a point he hasn't yet marked, he grabs his head with both hands, then stretches his arms as if trying to shake off the numbness; at last he draws the point on the shiny paper and stares at it for a while, he lays the pencil aside and squeezes his face with both hands, crumpling it like a sheet of paper that he's about to roll into a ball and toss into the wastebasket. I don't know why, but I think I can tell what question he's asking himself.

They've withdrawn the order to rush to the area where the *Sheffield* is, and we return to our patrol area around the islands. We still haven't been able to see them, no crew member has seen them, not even the co through the periscope.

A man floats and rocks inside his orange life jacket, face up on the surface of the sea. An albatross, as though recently arrived from a cloud, perches on his belly, the man opens his eyes and doesn't look at the bird on his body, but rather upward, he watches me, I see him as if I were suspended, as if I, too, were a heavy albatross, held up by the unusual afternoon chill. Now, after seeing his eyes, I recognize him: it's Medina. I didn't want to stay on land, he tells me, that's why I became a sailor and prepared to come in case you needed me, see? And the *Salta*, why not on the *Salta*? I ask him. It was being repaired, he explains, they said it had broken parts that made noise and so it stayed there, at least till we took off. But why the cruiser? I insist. Because that was what there was; the *Belgrano* was about to weigh anchor and I signed up as a volunteer, he replies, and the albatross turns calmly on its legs for a change of view, but in the end I never got to see the islands, we stayed here, on the way. Well, I reply, how do we know if we're going to see them? We'd have to win, and disembark, in order to do that, right? Yeah, sure, he says just as the albatross starts pecking at one of the silvery buckles on his orange jacket. And for us to win, we'd have to have torpedoes that work, I inform him. He opens his mouth as if to say something but then changes his mind and doesn't answer me. A piece of ice goes floating by; from here it looks as green as an emerald. Won't I see you anymore? I insist. You're seeing me right now, he answers, and this is all we know, neither of us can say how this story will play out. Then I notice that both of us are gently floating southward. Without saying another word, Medina closes his eyes, the albatross flaps its wings, pushes off with its legs, takes flight, and Medina's body begins to sink as if the albatross had been holding him up, the water covers him; I rise higher, and the visual line that joined us stretches out, until I can no longer make out his body, with all the water on top of him. So much water, so much that I have the feeling we're the first ever to have burst into this silent sea.

Someone touched the Magnavox, Gutiérrez announces in a loud voice, as if to make sure everyone in the command post area can hear him. Someone touched the Magnavox, he repeats, his eyes scanning everyone closest to him to see if some gesture might give them away; we've lost all the data we need to sail without crashing into a rock or the ocean floor. He takes a breath and remains staring at the machine; someone who doesn't know how it works and who has no reason to stick his hand in there, he goes on. The co, who has been watching him the whole time without intervening, suddenly walks up to Gutiérrez; takes a look at the screen Gutiérrez shows him, and gives the order to rise to periscope depth; Calm down, Gutiérrez, we'll work this out; he orders the engines turned off and the periscope raised, carefully observing to make sure there's nothing in sight; then he gives the order to raise the antenna in order to reload the data onto the Magnavox, while taking advantage of the opportunity to snorkel and tune in to Radio Carve or Colonia for news. Gutiérrez is still annoyed, they don't realize that not just anybody can touch this, because then all of us will be really fucked, not just the guy who touched it. The co looks at him, Gutiérrez lowers his head and mutters something softly as he walks past me toward the bow. I follow him to see what's happening. Nobrega pokes his head out of the galley, summoning him over with a crooked finger: *Che*, Gutiérrez, he says as he looks from side to side, I know who touched the Magnavox, but ssshhh, don't say anything … Gutiérrrez stares at him, waiting for the revelation. It was the co. What? whispers Gutiérrez, with contained surprise, you're crazy; I swear it's true, man, I saw him, but I didn't say anything because I thought he knew what he was doing, how was I supposed to imagine he was going to erase everything? C'mere, let's have a drink. I watch them go into the galley, then I return to the engine room; on the way I run into Albaredo, who was standing beside the radio and now also heads for the engine room; he gets there first, with me behind him. It seems the aircraft carrier *Hermes* broke down, he remarks to Soria, who's standing next to the engines. Really? asks Soria; So it seems, Albaredo replies, they heard about it on Radio Carve. And you believe the Uruguayans?

Soria prods him; You've gotta believe someone; I'm gonna get some juice, want any? Albaredo asks; No, thanks, I just had tea. If there's a storm today, it'll really shake up the guys on the aircraft carriers and keep them from operating with planes and choppers. They don't see us, nobody's seen us, nobody *can* see us, but they know we're here and they think we can do them damage. This ghostly presence of ours makes them nervous, and they're looking for us. Every so often you can hear the whirr of blades from a chopper that comes and goes, and that makes *us* nervous. Everything that happens seems to be duplicated in a grotesque symmetry: from the surface down, our sub; from the surface up, the helicopter. I look out toward the sonar zone. The bird is in its place; with a murmur it alerts one of the sonar operators. It returns to the same spot, flying over the sea once more, and now it pauses right above us, it doesn't give up. These Englishmen never give up, either; they seem tireless.

We've been settled on the bottom from the time we finished snorkeling early this morning till now, which is around five-thirty. I know it's five-thirty because Olivero just crossed paths with Polski at the bathroom door and asked him what time it was. I'm still lying in my bunk with my book; the animal has been startled by a noise that he listens to, unworried and smiling for the time being. Medrano passes the earphones to Cuéllar; Cuéllar nods. Then Medrano turns to the communications officer, but the animal suddenly stops smiling because it's true, there too you can hear the buzz and try to guess where it's coming from; they're calling us to our battle stations: the sonar operators have heard something, so I see feet wrapped in filthy socks and others in filthy sneakers filing down the corridor to the fortified enclosure, some toward the bow, others toward the stern; the boat begins to peel off from the bottom so that the sound can be plotted; the animal goes down the corridor toward the fortified enclosure, we're sailing to try to identify where the hydrophonic sound is coming from, the animal begins to listen, and yet what's happening is incomprehensible to him, he becomes annoyed and confused, blinded, he listens at the walls and on the floor, at the entryway and inside, everywhere he hears the same noise, everywhere, and how much time, how much tension does it take to constantly monitor an intermittent noise. Now Elizalde sits in front of the sonar equipment, relieving Medrano; the ear grows tired and loses its ability to identify sounds. Medrano walks toward the galley, the animal searches in the excavated earth, throwing clumps of dirt into the air that crumble and fall into the darkness of the den, but the noise isn't there; Medrano returns to the sonar equipment with two pitchers of coffee, which he passes to Cuéllar and Elizalde; the animal digs here and there, hurriedly, leaving piles of dirt that block the path and the line of sight. Medrano passes by me again and goes into the galley, exhausted; the animal falls asleep in a hole, mid-dig, one paw embedded in the earth. Medrano returns with another pitcher of coffee, Elizalde has passed the earphones to Medrano, who rests his cup next to the equipment; he puts on the earphones and confirms. Then he tells the communications officer and the communications officer tells the co. They call us to our battle stations. Someone remarks that the noise sounds like it's getting closer. Elizalde confirms the approximate position, the co orders us to rise to periscope level in order to identify the enemy, the Executive Officer comes out of his cabin with a glass of whiskey in his right hand, exchanges a glance with the CO, who at that moment is giving the order to raise the combat periscope, the Executive Officer stands there watching him, turns and goes back to his cabin, the CO grabs the periscope and turns it to scan the horizon, then steps aside so that the officer accompanying him can look, too; the officer observes, then he, too, steps aside and shakes his head no, the CO orders the periscope lowered, neither of them has seen anything on the surface of the sea, but the noise continues, so we descend to a lower level again, the noise can now be heard close by, the CO orders evasive maneuvers. Elizalde confirms that the target is making strategic moves and rejects the idea that it could be an animal. Gutiérrez receives an order from the gunnery officer and goes to the head to launch a false target; it's most likely a submarine, says someone nearby, there's frenzied activity at the command post, they're trying to figure out the exact position where the noise is coming from; it's very loud right now and can be heard without any equipment, Gutiérrez ejects another decoy. Alpha target very close, Medrano announces; we all hear the noise, growing louder and louder, toward the stern and getting closer, the CO gives the order to prepare to launch an anti-sub torpedo; I turn toward the bow, there's movement up there, a group of other guys open valves, flood compartments, close valves, Olivero confirms that the torpedo is ready; some men have started to reload torpedoes from the tubes; I turn toward the bow and see that Ghezzi is drawing a point on the brightly-lit map on the plotting chart; Data on targets adjusted, sir, Mainieri announces immediately; then the CO orders them to fire. Marini, who is sitting in front of the fire control computer, presses the launch button; from the bow Grunwald signals that the torpedo has been fired. No one speaks, everyone waits expectantly. Marini follows the data sent to the computer by the torpedo, the co checks his watch and calculates the minutes since it's been launched, pursuing the target we've never seen and may not ever see; I notice a bulge under a blanket, which has been left on the floor after taking the bunks apart; I squat, feel around, and discover that it's the jar of capers, four minutes, someone says in a half-whisper close by to my right, I look at my grimy socks, wiggle my covered toes a little, backward and forward, and wait for the explosion to be confirmed, five minutes, asserts the same hesitant voice beside me and still there's no news of the damned torpedo, I keep moving my toes and my toes start to move on their own again, but I still can't feel them, and anyway I'm starting to get used to this lack of feeling, six minutes, look, it's the *Endurance*, someone to my left whispers boldly, do you remember when the *Endurance* was in Mar del Plata? Imagine, we ate at an *asado* with those guys, seven minutes, they recount to my right, and now we may have blown them all to fucking hell, those same guys who sat right opposite us at the table at the Submarine Force's barbecue, shhh, someone a little farther forward hisses, placing his fingers against his lips like a picture of a nurse at a hospital, eight minutes, the voice announces again, and I try to recall if there was a picture of a nurse calling for silence at the place where they took me after that breakdown, but I can't remember anything, it was right in the engine room when everything went black and I was struck with this forgetfulness of mine, nine minutes, the voice announces, softly but firmly, I remember what that boat was like when we first saw it, the whispering voice goes on, what the *Endurance* was and is, you know? And how those Gringos drank whiskey, the good stuff, their own, did anybody visit me when I was in the hospital, if, in fact, I ever was? Ten minutes, hey, is that the sub that's looking for us, those dudes could've fucked us up instead of us fucking them, the voice goes on, and I don't remember, I want to remember something after the breakdown but I just don't remember, maybe someone aboard the *Endurance* is saying: Do you remember those Argentine submariners who welcomed us with an *asado*? How do you say *asado* in English? I bet those dudes never ate anything as good as that *asado* we made for them, it melts in your mouth! And how would you say in English this sensation of not feeling your feet, this wanting to remember and not being able to? Eleven minutes, who could possibly have thought of all this? Of sticking all of us in this, a tube full of Argentines here, a slightly bigger tube full of Englishmen over there, or right here, an endless, frightening sea, damaged, and … twelve minutes, the voice on my right confirms and suddenly the explosion, a tremendous burst that rocks the water and our ship as well. Sunk? We all keep silent, grabbing hold of whatever each of us can; the sonarmen, alert, wait for the temblor to pass so they can confirm what's happened, using hydrophonic sound; no one moves from their spot: the voice to my left whispers, could it have been just the *Endurance*? Elizalde passes the earphones to Cuéllar; Cuéllar nods. Elizalde announces: The hydrophonic sound has disappeared, sir. The second in command opens his cabin door, comes out of his isolation, looks forward, then turns his gaze aft and heads for the command post. I return to my book; the animal has awakened and is now using dirt to cover the holes he made a while ago when searching for the noise. However, the noise that invades his den hasn't stopped, and the animal seems confused. I raise my eyes from the book; the sonar operators are still listening; we don't yet know what our torpedo has hit. Everything is blindness here.

They call us again to cover our combat posts, one-thirty in the morning, goddammit, says Gómez alongside me as he stands and smooths out his damp, wrinkled overalls, what's going on with those English, don't they ever sleep? he complains, walking away toward the torpedo area. Although my legs have become numb, I stand, too—not without a certain clumsiness—and start out for the engine room; Soria, Torres, and Albaredo are already there, but I stick around anyway. Albaredo goes out for a while; Soria and Torres look at each other, one of them bearded, the other clean-shaven, from inside their life jackets; they look like reflections of one another in a warped mirror. Albaredo comes tiptoeing back, the noise has returned, he explains in a whisper; What noise, asks Soria, also in a very quiet voice, passing his right hand over his head; The same one we heard before we launched the torpedo, Albaredo replies; But, what does that mean? Are we the same as before? No way of knowing, but there's no propeller noise, so maybe it's a swarm of krill. And then a memory hits me like an avalanche: once, on the *Piedrabuena*, someone lit a reflector on the stern to fish and the krill came toward the light, it appeared before the light as if blooming from nothing, you couldn't see it because of how tiny it was, but minutes after lighting the reflector we found ourselves in the middle of a stain so red and thick that it looked like the boat had been stabbed and was bleeding, slowly and merrily, on the dark sea that moonless night.

We haven't bathed in so long that the smell clinging to us must be awful, a mix of old grime and diesel oil, but we're so covered in it that we don't even smell it. Everyone goes around with full beards, some longer, some shorter, Soria not at all, but you don't see anybody scratching himself anymore; the itching days have passed. Maceda, the second in command, walks by me and stops—a few steps before reaching the periscope and without taking his eyes off what's happening at the command post—to talk to one of the officers. His mouth is a slit in the middle of the bush of reddish hair of his beard; he gestures, emphasizing his words with his hands, I have the impression he's trying to convince him of something. It's dawn, comments someone nearby, and the murmur reaches me crossing this spatial silence that the boat seems to be wrapped in when it's settled at the bottom with the engines turned off. Now suddenly I see myself in my white school smock, reciting: *At the bottom of the sea there's a glass house*, with a motion of my right hand drawing an imaginary sea bed for the rest of my schoolmates, *to an avenue of coral* ... but I don't know what coral is and I feel like I can't go on, Señorita Elsa looks at me and her pink-painted lips stretch into an endless smile, and I wonder if she knows what coral is, and then I forget how the rest of the poem goes, my classmates look at one another, I repeat it from the beginning to see if that way I'll be able to continue: *At the bottom of the sea there's a house* ... but no, after the coral there are no more words, they've been erased, and everyone that lives in them has disappeared, too, Señorita Elsa's not there anymore, in her place is the Hyena, with his everlasting smile, his shaved face and his white scarf, he orders me to continue because everyone is lined up on deck waiting for me to recite so they can weigh anchor, so there I go again: *At the bottom of the sea there's a* ... *metal house*, I stammer, but at last I go on, a blind whale with its belly full of Jonahs, the water surrounds them, the abyss surrounds them, and some algae is about to entangle itself around their heads. I stop talking, lower my eyes, smooth out my smock, the Hyena applauds loudly and emotionally, he applauds and applauds and applauds, and a dense fog descends over all of us.

This numbness in some parts of my body is very strange, yet here I am, walking once more toward the table at the bow, with my beat-up little book in my right hand. Grunwald and Heredia are drinking juice; under these conditions you have to add a little sugar; I sit down at the table, open the book to the page where I had left off reading; the animal has decided to stop wandering along the corridors in search of a new source of noise, instead devoting himself to noticing the ugly holes, the nasty cracks he's made in the walls. The Executive Officer told Nobrega that it was suicidal to go on like that with the torpedoes not working, mutters Grunwald in front of me, and he walks around saying it would be better to go back. Yes, but he's not the CO, he's not the one who decides, replies Heredia, who's sitting at the head of the table, to Grunwald's right; suddenly the animal decides to remain in some random place and concentrate on listening; I know, says Grunwald, and we're here to fight, but the way things are ... he touches his chin with a gesture that emphasizes this unexpected silence generated by the interrupted sentence and the confusion that seems to have invaded it. Just let the Executive Officer keep talking, adds Heredia, no one's going to follow him, at least I'm not, even if I'm dying to meet my son, how am I supposed to look the kid in the face if ... And I keep on making more useless discoveries, confesses the animal in his den, and it's just that sometimes he thinks that the noise has stopped because there are long pauses. I'm distracted for a moment and cast a sidelong glance at the black curtain that separates us from the aft bunks, the few bunks that were left standing, and underneath I spy the toes of my boots, the black dent. I keep on making more useless discoveries, the animal says, and he starts to believe it would be better to find someone without cracks to confide in. Olivero has moved over to the table, appearing suddenly, nimbly, and silently, as usual; he sits down beside me and pours himself a glass of juice. And what he wants to do, he can't do alone, Heredia continues, he can't do it without us; did you get the message, too? asks Olivero; Grunwald and Heredia nod yes; the first thing that needs to be done now, my animal thinks, is to inspect the den's defense systems. Suddenly I lift my eyes from the book; the conversation distracts me and I don't feel like reading anymore; I close the book, and just when I'm about to rest my hand on Olivero's shoulder in a kind of greeting, he anticipates my movement, smiles at me, and says Thanks. For what? asks Grunwald; I wasn't talking to you, Olivero replies; Grunwald looks at Heredia, Heredia shrugs; it seems like being locked up in here is affecting all of us, Grunwald remarks; Olivero gives me a smile as he looks me in the eye, blood is pulsing in my ears and for some crazy reason I think of coral again. They call us to our battle stations; we all get up immediately, the sub lists to one side, we start to peel off from the bottom, we leave the table, and everyone heads for his assigned place: Olivero, Grunwald, and Heredia uphill toward the bow, the torpedo area; me, downhill and sternward, toward the engine room. The jar of capers rolls past me, getting ahead of me; I follow it with my gaze as I advance; I see it stop right before the co's cabin door, against a rolled-up blue blanket that's lying on the floor, I reach the jar and now I'm the one who's gaining the lead and leaving it behind; as I pass through the sonar area, I find out that the sonar operators have picked up a hydrophonic sound; now the co orders us to set a course toward the enemy in order to shorten the distance and shoot off a torpedo; now we're level and at full speed to try to catch up with it, but with the engine malfunction, we're moving very slowly, and we all know that unless the enemy ship slows down or stops, it will get away. I enter the engine room and someone comes up behind me; they say it's a sure thing they're gonna shell Puerto Argentino or Puerto Darwin; a voice catches me off guard, and then I turn and see that it's Torres who has just walked in. Stop the engines, the voice of the engineering officer bursts in, getting ahead of Torres; Engines stopped; understood, sir, replies Albaredo, and immediately Torres and Soria obey the order; engines are stopped, Albaredo reports to the engineering officer, who now withdraws; for sure we'll wait here till it comes back, Soria declares softly, and here it won't get away from us; yeah, but by the time it gets back, it'll have done some damage, Albaredo replies, just as softly; we ought to have caught up with it, but the engines we've got that are still operable aren't enough. I leave the engine room, slip behind the sonar operators, who remain on alert, since another enemy ship might appear at any moment. Egea emerges from the galley with Gutiérrez behind him, both carrying plates of food in their hands, they pass in front of me on their way sternward, it's rice with tomatoes, I confirm, you've got to take advantage of this pause in the action to eat, while we wait for the ship that got away from us to come back, and maybe some other one, as well. For now,

I return to the table at the bow in order to read for a while; I run into Polski, who's coming out of the NCO's head, he takes a few steps forward, goes into the galley, and asks what there is to eat, I keep going, the jar of capers is no longer in the place where it had gotten stuck, it must have rolled somewhere else, I reach the bow, but the table is occupied, everyone's already eating, after all, those are the only places where you can sit on something besides the damp floor, so I take a couple of steps backward and sit on the pile of clothing and blankets where I've been resting lately. Look where the Remington was, Polski grumbles, coming out of the galley as he aims for a corner next to the CO's cabin and picks up the little typewriter. I take the book out of my overalls; the dampness of the atmosphere has softened it, like my hands and everyone else's, which, from lack of sun, are also beginning to look greenish-white.

Air circulation has stopped, and the absence of that faint, familiar, constant noise throws me into a state of alarm and awakens me; I sit up and look toward the sonar; the three sonar operators are there, a sign that they've detected something. It seems to be coming from the two ships that were on their way to Puerto Argentino earlier, comments Heredia as he crosses in front of me, loping toward the torpedo area. I stand and listen to the CO order a course that will cut off the enemy's retreat and also issue an order to pass out life jackets. Olivero is in charge of the life jackets, which are stored at the bow, in the row of cots that were left assembled, and now he starts handing them out, starting at the bow and moving toward the area of the disassembled cots where I am—I don't want one, I don't think they'll do us any good if a torpedo hits us—he keeps distributing them near the command post, all the officers put on their life jackets, the CO refuses with a shake of his head—he hasn't used one in all the time we've been crossing and he's not about to use one now, and he heads for the periscope, most likely in order to spot enemy targets. Olivero walks toward the fire control computer, about to hand a life jacket to Marini, who he hasn't spoken to since they boarded the sub that foggy Sunday when we weighed anchor. When he reaches the computer, he stops next to the seat Marini occupies at the monitor; he taps him on the shoulder, Marini turns his head and watches as Olivero unties a little bag he wears knotted to his belt. They're chocolate bars, Olivero says to him, try not to get them wet, they'll come in handy if we have to disembark; Marini stands up and keeps staring at him, he seems surprised, as if he doesn't exactly know what to do; suddenly he gives Olivero a hug and hears Olivero say: What assholes we were, right? I hear him, too, and stand there watching how they disentangle themselves from that embrace and how Olivero hands Marini the lifejacket, which Marini accepts with a smile. Now Olivero continues with the distribution, moving toward the sonar area; then he'll go on toward the control compartment, and finally toward the engine room. The night is too dark, says someone passing nearby on his way to the officers' cabin, his face concealed by the periscope. Since it's not my shift in the engine room, I set out for the bow; Grunwald and Heredia are once again sitting on the bench near the torpedo launchers, both of them in lifejackets. Grunwald is wearing the little wire glasses, Heredia has a rosary dangling from his neck; Olivero shows up, having finished handing out the lifejackets; we're within firing range now, between the two ships, an ideal location, he remarks; it looks like one of them is a missile boat, and just as he says it I see the dead: they're floating in the frozen, gray sea, around twenty of them, and behind them is a seriously damaged Argentine ship, fuming its defeat into the equally gray sky. Movement in the torpedo area jostles me out of these imaginings, two lights flicker on the screen next to the torpedo launchers, number one and number eight; that means we need to prepare two SST-4 torpedoes for launching; Olivero and somebody else flood tubes one and eight, the air comes out of the tubes and a little water spills out, the outside door opens; they're probably working at the command post to coordinate data, another light goes on, indicating that the doors of torpedo launchers one and eight are open, Olivero activates one of the lights, then the other, to notify the command post that the torpedoes are ready. The CO issues the order to fire number one, I imagine Marini at this moment pressing the computer button to fire it off, you can hear the torpedo's engine revving up, but seconds go by and the computer doesn't fire, while a couple of men work quickly to stop it, the CO gives the order to fire the other readied torpedo, the engine starts up, you can hear the buzz it makes as it slides along the torpedo launcher, its fall into the water, the slightest pause, the beginning of its trajectory. Luckily the torpedo that failed has been deactivated, or it would have exploded, along with us, here inside. Grunwald looks at his watch through his empty glasses, Heredia, in turn, stares at him gazing at the watch, Olivero observes both of them; I turn toward the bow and see the rest of the crew looking this way, toward the valves of the activated torpedo launcher, their eyes fixed on it, as if by all of them looking at the same point they might achieve a concentration of will that could hit the target and explode these unpredictable torpedoes that up to now have done nothing but fail us. One minute, Grunwald shouts, and after that brief phrase, silence; a couple of meters forward, the cook, sitting on the floor, reads another comic book, and I think that in one of the drawings I can see the floating dead, and in the panel following that one, a burning ship, THE ISLA DE LOS ESTADOS SINKS, announce the upper-case letters that I can't quite see from here, but can guess; two minutes, Grunwald says, Heredia clasps the cross on his rosary with one hand and I find myself looking at the poster Nobrega drew a few days ago, from there the woman looks back at me, framed by her long, blond hair; the cook turns the page to keep reading, I hear "the torpedo cut the wire, sir," over the fire control console, two minutes thirty, Grunwald pronounces; it's too soon, Olivero mutters in a very faint voice, stating what we all know, or maybe he didn't really say it, he's thought it but kept his mouth shut; in this state of silence and these brushes with death, it sometimes happens that I hear everything that the others seem to hear, the others' voices, what they're going to say and never say. Then there's a crash of sheet metal, as if someone is striking a giant gong, the gong from the Rank Organization films I used to watch with my father when I was a boy, about war, about con-BOYS, as my old man used to call cowboys, with an "n" and stressing the last syllable, but there's no explosion: the torpedo has hit the target without exploding; fucking torpedoes, everyone shouts with their mouths closed, they shout it in their heads, in the midst of a sea of curses, motherfucking torpedoes, to be here and be unable to do anything, to be here and accomplish nothing, nothing. Somebody next to me snorts the air of his disappointment; a tear rolls down the cook's face; he stops it with his blue shirt cuff and conceals the action by turning his eyes to the magazine again; Ships retreating, sir, Elizalde announces from the sonar area, and we all know—even though nobody says so—that it will be impossible to catch up with them. In any case that doesn't make us feel any better: even if these two ships don't attack us, they'll report our position and soon they'll come after us.

I bring my book over to the table at the bow, settle myself in, open it, but instead of reading, I sit there watching what Almaraz is writing in his black notebook: the CO sent a wire where he explained everything. This afternoon they replied, ordering us to return. We're to arrive at Puerto Belgrano on the nineteenth at 2 AM. The Executive Officer must be happy we're going back, Heredia remarks; I, on the other hand, am really angry that we're leaving just like that; Nobrega pulls up to the table with paper and pencil in hand, sits in the empty place that was left next to Heredia, but that's where they're fixing the computer and the engine, so we go back. Soon those Brits will get what's coming to them! Grunwald promises, smiling; I don't know, I think we all have that bitter taste in our mouths, right? pipes up Almaraz, who's stopped writing and now closes his black notebook; Nobrega gets ready to sketch; Yeah, Heredia says, we're returning with the feeling that all the stuff we went through was totally useless; Nobrega raises his eyes from the sheet of paper and stares at it without offering an opinion; But we'll never know it, locked up in here with no communication, we'll soon find out what things are like, says Grunwald; Nobrega draws a line that twists and straightens and twists and folds back on itself; deep down, I think we all know what things are like, says Almaraz, and adds, turning to Heredia: At least think of this, you're going to meet your son, and we're going to see our loved ones, our families, and in a few days ... now Nobrega retouches the line, giving it thickness and depth, as if he were drawing the wall of an endless labyrinth; Sure, sure, of course, Heredia replies, but first we have to get back, right? Then I return to my book; the animal complains that he no longer understands his earlier plan, he can't find anything reasonable in it; Almaraz stashes the notebook in the pocket of his overalls and gets up from the table; Nobrega's labyrinth becomes compact and gray; once more the animal abandons his labors as well as his eavesdropping task, he doesn't want to discover that the noise is growing louder, he puts everything aside in order to try to calm his inner conflict; They'll be looking for us, no doubt about it, Grunwald announces; meanwhile, the animal doesn't know what he's looking for, possibly just trying to buy himself a little more time. We're going back, and I wonder how you can return to a place you no longer remember; ever since I woke up that day of the noise, everything seems to be limited to what happens in here, plus a few scraps of the past that my memory arbitrarily cuts short. Nobrega's labyrinth is now dense and indecipherable, and it looks like it's going to lift off from the paper.

We're sailing northward, always submerged and alert to every noise; we have to cross a zone we imagine to be loaded with English ships and subs, they've mapped a defeat for us that starts in the Malvinas and goes straight north, near Necochea, and from there we'll have to go back hugging the coast, returning southward as far as Puerto Belgrano. Since we can't shoot off those worthless torpedoes anymore, the co has given the order to set up the bunks again, so several people are busy securing them in place and then picking up the mats, sheets, and blankets that are still on the floor. I gather up some sheets to help out a little, but they fall from my hands a couple of times, so I give up and leave to keep from getting in the way. I walk toward the torpedo area and sit on the bench opposite the instrument panel, I sit there staring at my hands, without feeling them; I bring my right hand to my eyes, raise it, and move it to my head; when we were cabin boys we didn't wear sailors' caps because we were too new and didn't even know how to salute; whenever a superior passed by, we had to put our hand against our head to pretend we were covered; everybody was superior to us at the Naval Mechanics' School, even the pigeons, and there were enough of those to be a real pain. Now I can't feel my hand against my head, I move it down to stop it, with the palm turned inward, right before my eyes, and what I see is a map of slightly faded grooves.

Meanwhile the operator snorkels and some of the others take the opportunity to listen to Radio Carve. It seems an English warship was attacked by a torpedo that hit but didn't explode, more or less in the area where we were; it might have been the torpedo we thought was lost. The others say they hear that the aircraft carrier *Hermes* won't be received for repair in Curaçao; they also heard that the prisoners from the *Santa Fe* arrived today in Argentina from the South Georgia Islands. But we won't know anything, really, till we get there. I think of Mancuso again. It won't be long now, the others say; I'm sleepy nearly all the time, and, even though I sleep a lot, the days of this return trip seem long. So, to keep myself entertained, when this semi-permanent drowsiness I've fallen into lets up or a few moments, I go back to reading my book, the ridiculous digressions of the animal in his den, who lately has caught on to the fact that the other threatening thing, which he doesn't understand and which he sometimes calls a noise and sometimes an animal, seems to have a plan whose meaning he can't figure out; then he surrounds the noise, digging circles around it because he understands that the fact that the noise comes back louder each time means that the circles are growing narrower and that the other thing is coming ever closer.

Today is Navy Day, one of the others remarks, and that phrase—coming from nearby, though I can't say exactly from where—rouses me; we're nearly opposite Necochea, the voice adds, so now we're starting to turn south. I had fallen asleep with the book open on my chest; now I close it and stand with the intention of getting up and walking a little to see what's going on; we'll be emerging shortly and will travel on the surface till we arrive in port. Book in hand, I gather momentum and scramble down from my bunk just as the jar of capers, which obviously had been in my bed and which I might have accidentally pushed with my numb feet, rolls with a dull noise into a jacket that's fallen from another bunk, and comes to a halt at the feet of someone passing by. This jar again? It's a miracle it didn't break, says one of the others, startled by the noise and poking his head out from a bunk on the other side of the corridor; it's been rolling around from one place to another; why doesn't somebody take it to the galley? I did, replies the guy who had been walking down the corridor a moment ago and who now bends down and grabs the jar; I took it there but it showed up again somewhere or other, he adds as he heads to the galley with the jar and disappears behind the door. At that very moment, a few steps closer to me, someone comes out of the head bare-chested, a grease-stained towel rolled around his waist, on his way to the bunks, crossing paths with another guy going by, also bare-chested, but with a dry towel—or rather, as dry as a towel or anything else can be in here—a towel, at any rate, rolled around *his* waist. Most likely they've given him permission, and water, to wash himself, as we've nearly arrived. The grubbier one has disappeared behind the bathroom door; the recently bathed guy rummages through his belongings, I imagine in search of a clean change of clothes. I'll stay here, says Soria, who has just drawn the curtains of his bunk and is now sitting up there, legs dangling, for the first time in weeks without his life vest; with all the filth I'm carrying around, I need liters and liters of water and at least one packet of Camello detergent. He pauses, and as nobody says anything, he continues: Besides, I've run out of clean clothes, I've got that new shirt they gave me when we left, it was so stiff that the first day I tried it on, it hurt my neck and I had to take it off. The guy who came out of the bathroom and is now changing, stares at him as he balances on one leg and sticks the other into a seemingly clean pair of blue overalls; he looks at Soria as if he's trying to make a comment he can't quite express in words; then Soria explains, in reply to that question, which didn't need to be pronounced: That's fine for you because you're nice and comfortable sitting in front of the radio, but those of us who are in the engine room, stinking of diesel and with greasy hands . . . for us a little bit of water makes no difference. At last, taking long strides, I set out for the table at the bow; with all this commotion going on at the head, the place is pretty calm: Almaraz writes in his black notebook, Nobrega takes down the poster he drew a few weeks ago, which someone hung next to the torpedo indicator panel;

he folds it in quarters and returns aft, possibly to take down
the other poster, which at this point is no longer necessary.

I open my eyes, I'm in my bunk, there's a faint glow from
the night lights, and so I realize that it must be nighttime
outside. I lie still in bed, a slight panting invades my space
and I think I can tell that it's coming from the bunk above
mine; this is another way I can see that we're heading back:
people have started to think about things nobody thought
about during those dangerous days. The panting grows in
rhythm and intensity, and I wonder if I'm the only one who
hears it; some of the bunk curtains are closed, others are open;
I can see a few of the others from here, they're sound asleep; I
might be the only one who hears the sighs, the slight friction
produced by the regular movement of the mattress against
the upper bunk, like an owl's shush, a shh, shh that repeats,
shh, shh, and repeats. I close my eyes and little by little the
noise turns into light, a light that grows brighter and more
enveloping, and then I see the sub as if I were outside, flying
above it, it's skimming along the surface of the water, the
crests of the waves forming to port and starboard glisten with
phosphorescent edges that contrast with the black boat and
the black sky, a milky wake that shines like a beam from an
immeasurable lighthouse. I plunge into the light, I am the ship
itself, making its way among the waters, through the pure,
intense radiance; I let myself be carried along, as if the light
sustains me, floating above it effortlessly, but now, suddenly,
the sea recovers its dense, ordinary appearance and I am no
longer the boat, I'm a man out here, standing in the conning
tower, a man who turns his head and can see behind the boat
and behind himself, all the way to the horizon, how the sky

reflects the luminescence of the water that remains farther and farther behind us, slowing yielding to the darkness. I open my eyes, the night navigation light outlines my bunk and I realize that the panting has ended; a little creak—which I recognize as the curtain of the upper bunk being opened—suggests that the guy up there is going to come down; now I see a pair of feet wrapped in dark socks dangling a few inches from my face, but I choose to close my eyes in order to recapture that image I had of the outside. I try and try, but I can't do it; it seems there's nothing left; I persist, but I can't get back, there's not even a trace left of that calming, enveloping light, only the black void of what just a moment ago were empty glimmers.

I've just awakened, curled up in a ball, I stretch to loosen up, retrieve the book from under my pillow, stick it in my overall pocket and get down from the bunk with some difficulty. No sooner do I start walking than I run into Almaraz and notice his long, thick beard full of white fuzz; a moment's hesitation and then we're both on our way, him heading aft and me forward, now I cross paths with Polski, also with his beard full of fuzz, and automatically I bring my hand to my face: maybe I have a beard full of fuzz too, but I don't feel my beard or my hand; I'll have to go into the head and look at myself in the scratched steel mirror, but I'd rather keep going forward and see if I can read for a while. A couple of men are there, around the table, I walk over to them, make a place for myself, and sit down. Anybody know where this book came from? one of them asks, waving a tattered, yellowed book, identical to mine, in his right hand, so identical that reflexively I pat my overall pocket to make sure it's still there, but I don't feel it; then I wonder: If it's the same book, how the hell did it get there if I was so sure I had put it in my pocket? Let me see, says another one, reaching out his hand so the guy who had waved it in the air can pass it to him; now that I've got it closer to me I see that it's the one I've been reading, the one about the animal in the den; the guy who received it flips through the pages and remarks: You can't understand this thing, what language is it in? Grunwald says it's German, the first guy replies, even though he doesn't understand anything, he says he's sure it's German. How could it be written in German, I say to myself, if I don't know any German and I'm reading it; then Olivero comes over from the torpedo launchers, takes the book from the one who's been leafing through it; to Groppa, the oldest NCO of the crew, the book came in one of the containers that held submarine parts, Olivero explains, when they sent it from Germany to assemble it in the Buenos Aires shipyards, one of the assemblers found it and decided that if it had come with the boat, it would stay on the boat, so from the time they began assembling the *San Luis,* the book has never left here. And does anybody know what it's about? asks the guy who was waving the book in the air a few moments ago; I could explain it to them perfectly, but I keep quiet and listen: they say an officer who knew a little German read part of it once, Olivero adds, on a campaign, but I don't know who the officer was, or if he said what it was about, it's just a rumor, but the book stays on board for luck; it goes around and around, from hand to hand, from stem to stern and from stern to stem, it's part of the boat, all boats hide a secret and this must be ours, Olivero concludes, as he lays the book on the table and returns to his post beside the torpedo launchers. The others who were seated stand up, carrying their empty glasses, but I stay here, watching the book; I sit down at the table, open it and search—with difficulty because of how clumsy my hands are—for the page where I had left off reading, German, I don't know what they're talking about. I start to read: deep silence, says the animal, how lovely it is to be here, no one is worried about my den, each one has his tasks, which have nothing to do with me.

We're approaching Puerto Belgrano, everything on board is movement, preparations, and enormous expectations, as nobody knows what we're going to find outside, nobody knows where the rest of the fleet might be, how they're managing, how things back there on the islands have been going, when our computer will be fixed so we can set sail again. The only thing we know is that ever since we've adapted to the new sense of balance that being at sea all this time has inflicted on our bodies, for a day or two it'll be hard for us to walk on *terra firma*, to regain the stability the others have, those who stayed behind. The same thing will happen with the light, after so many days of being closed up inside under fluorescent bulbs, the sunlight will be unbearable, it'll take us a few days to get used to it. Thirty-nine days of patrol and eight hundred sixty-four hours of immersion, Heredia remarks as he passes in front of me on his way to the torpedo area. Some people calculate everything, I say to myself, and I see Soria heading astern, toting a broom; I follow him with my eyes; he stops at the command post and says something to Officer Rabellini, who in turn walks toward the CO and almost certainly passes on what Soria, waiting for a reply, has told him. The CO nods; Rabellini returns to the spot where Soria, broom in hand, waits for him; he motions to Gómez, who's coming out of the galley, Gómez goes over to Rabellini, who seems to explain something to him or give him an order; then Soria hands the broom to Gómez, who takes it in his right hand, walks toward the periscope area, and stops beneath the hatch leading to the sail; the sub has slowed down, one of the others opens the hatch, and Gómez starts to climb up, broom in hand, till he disappears inside the hole that leads upward and outward; that's what they told us, says Grunwald, wearing his fake wire glasses, to tie the broom to the conning tower to show we've swept the area, so that's where Gómez is going. But we didn't hit anybody, Nobrega protests as he passes by: well, yeah, but the Brits did beat it out of there a couple of times; we messed things up for them—with no results, Grunwald argues. Yeah, I'm not denying that, Nobrega agrees and continues on his way; then I remember my boots, decide to go look for them and organize my things a little. I reach the table at the bow, where some of the others are eating, I draw open the curtain slightly that separates the bunks from this sector. Polski is asleep; he's really tall, and since he doesn't fit anywhere, he sleeps on the diagonal, half lying across the cot, with his feet sticking out into the corridor; there are my boots, I stand there for a moment looking at the indentation that distinguishes them, I grab them together by the upper edge, pinching them with my right hand, close the curtain again, and stop to look at the others, but it seems they're looking away so as not to bother me, so I continue on to my bunk, trying to remember where I could have left the book I want to finish reading; I cross paths with Grunwald, who's heading forward again, and Gutiérrez, who's coming from the command post, grumbling under his breath and carrying a ream of fresh paper in his hands; I leave the boots on my bunk; it looks like docking maneuvers are about to begin. I climb into my bed, shove the boots aside and down toward my feet, find the book tumbled among the covers, hide it under the pillow, and close my eyes with the illusion that on this return everything might return to the way it was in the old days.

We're entering Puerto Belgrano, on batteries, in complete silence; it's nighttime, and from below I see the black hole of the sky outlining the open hatch up there. The co, Ghezzi, Maineri, and Polski are up at the sail, the rest are all down here, not yet feeling the fresh air from outside. Someone goes down the ladder, judging by his great height, it must be Polski; yes, it's Polski, who's just come down and is heading sternward. I follow him, he stops next to Almaraz, who's acting as maneuvers helmsman to steer us into port. Everybody's here, Polski says; Everybody who? asks Almaraz; The whole damn combat fleet; Really? Yeah, even the aircraft carrier; The aircraft carrier? Almaraz repeats in disbelief; the aircraft carrier, and listen to this, the *Salta*! But how can that be? Why? I don't know, Polski replies angrily, but what I do know is that we're the only dumb asses who are still here. I return to my bed, I don't want to keep listening. Soria passes me and goes into the galley; now, without his life vest, he looks different. When I get to my bunk I see that my boots aren't there, and I don't feel like keeping up with that game anymore, I forget the whole business, climb up and lie down; from the row of bunks on the other side of the corridor a whisper reaches me, Cuéllar has the Bible open and is moving his lips; I close my eyes, trying to remember my mother's face, but I can't.

I wake up. I don't know how long I was asleep, but it's obvious that the boat is stopped and silent. I have the feeling no one's around, that I'm here alone. I try to stand, but I still have that strange lack of feeling all through my body; I stand up, look around: the bunks are empty. I walk toward the forward ladder, look up, and see that the hatch is open. The sky is still dark, so I assume it's still nighttime, or it's a different night, how can I tell with that heavy drowsiness I feel. I climb up slowly, reach one of the last rungs and look out through the round opening of the hatch: all the others are on deck, many of them smoking—I see the little red lights of their cigarette tips coming and going from their invisible mouths into the night; some of them are talking quietly. The aircraft carrier and the other boats that surround us look huge and are thick and black, like a deep hole. A voice orders the men to come down, saying we're going to spend the night here because we still don't have permission to disembark. Some of them complain as they start moving, they're a bunch of shadows among the shadows. I start to come down in order to leave the ladder free for the others to follow. I head for my bunk; from behind me comes the sound of boots landing on the narrow metal rungs, boots descending, voices entering. I climb into my bed, some people go by silently, walking astern, others are still complaining as they scramble into their bunks and get comfortable. I'm already in bed; little by little things settle down; in the lower bunk of the opposite row, Cuéllar closes his eyes and clutches the Bible resting on his chest. My lids feel heavy and I drift off to sleep.

A noisy sonar ping awakens me, awakens us, I jump out of my bunk, the others do the same, no doubt each one of them thinking about covering his combat post. Then someone stops and says: Guys, the ladder is open, we're not sailing, we're in

Puerto Belgrano. The confusion freezes us in place: no one dares to say or do anything. Nobrega, who apparently went outside to smoke or look around, is climbing down the ladder and explains loudly that what we heard was a sonar ping, produced by one of the corvettes that are in port to keep enemy divers away from the dock. It's just five o'clock, says someone over there. Little by little everyone returns to their bed. And so do I.

We're in formation, standing against the bunks, on both sides of the central corridor and toward the stern, skirting the periscopes in silence, because they've just announced that the Commander of the Submarine Force, the Hyena, is in Puerto Belgrano and is coming to greet us. Then we see our Commander, standing in the torpedo area, raise his face toward the ladder at the bow. A pair of shiny new boots appears in everybody's line of sight, and behind them a pair of spotless white pants, without a single wrinkle, and then a navy blue gabardine jacket and a shaved nape and a white cap that turns to reveal that face with its eternal, familiar grimace of a smile. Then, I don't know why, I get the idea of looking at my feet, maybe because the Hyena's gesture reminds me of the dent in my boots, I look at my feet and realize I'm not wearing shoes; all my shipmates have changed clothes, but I'm still dressed in the same pair of overalls and grubby socks. The situation embarrasses me, so I try not to look at the Hyena or at our Commander, I know it seems like a ridiculous thing to do, that it's impossible that no one will notice my socks among so many pairs of boots, but I do it anyway, I lower my head and avoid looking at them, hoping they'll continue on their way and ignore me, that the Hyena will give his welcome speech and get done with this stuff once and for all, even though it occurs to me that the best thing might have been to explode into a thousand pieces and never come back; that way we'd be victims or heroes, not this living proof of something that doesn't work, of something wrong, of failure. The Hyena keeps talking, I pay no attention to what he's saying, but he keeps talking, out of the corner of my eye I see everybody looking in his direction, I don't want to listen, so I concentrate on trying to remember something, whatever, something that happened after the day of my incident, something from my recovery, something from the hospital, but there's no hospital, there's no recovery, there's nothing till that day when I woke up on the floor of the engine room; and there's nothing now, either, except this jumble of words flying up and down the ship, trying to get into our ears.

The speech ended a while ago, and the Hyena has left us; some men went to have dinner on the *Santiago del Estero*, which left Mar del Plata after we took off and just barely managed, without submerging, to get here; at this point she's our mother ship and she welcomes us aboard to eat. Other men—those who had dinner at the first seating—are asleep; still others went up on deck, to smoke, no doubt, everybody smokes now, those who always smoked, those who had given it up, those who never did it; everybody smokes except Soria and me. Polski is walking forward now, from my bunk I can see him climb the ladder and disappear; you can hear voices coming from there, and suddenly, maybe when they discover that a lot of guys are sleeping, they lower their voices; a couple of men climb down and head for their bunks. I can't fall asleep, so I decide to follow behind Polski: I climb the ladder and remain standing on the top rung, looking out on deck through the hatch opening. Polski is outside, with his head raised like an animal sniffing the night; someone in a long black cape approaches, not a crew member from the *San Luis*, and gives Polski a hug that looks intense and emotional: What are you doing? What do you need? Do you guys need anything? the new arrival asks, moving away a little with his arms extended, but keeping his hands on Polski's shoulders; I can't exactly see, but I think I recognize Morán's voice, the electrician from our replacement crew, who stayed behind here in Puerto Belgrano. Smokes, Polski replies in his thick, hoarse voice, and that word, "smokes," echoes in the air as if it had been pronounced in a cave. I'm coming, says Morán, who's just broken the embrace, turns, and moves away till he blends into the shadows. Someone else approaches along the deck, greets Polski, and gets in line for the hatch, so I move aside to let him climb down. Now I look in Polski's direction again, a black shape comes closer with something dangling from his hand; it's Morán, wrapped in his black cape and advancing toward Polski; he stops, picks up the package with both hands; it looks like a carton of cigarettes; Forty-Three Seventy Darks, says Morán; and I know they'll be too strong for Polski, who I've always seen smoking Jockey Club Lights. Morán signals with his hand and Polski follows him, I follow them too—but with my eyes—and watch them go down to the dock, walk a few steps till I lose them in a blur of darkness and then see them reemerge in the shimmery, hazy circle of light silhouetted against the pavement by a street lamp. I hear voices, the group that had gone to the *Santiago del Estero* for dinner is returning, so I go down to make room for them and stand next to the torpedoes, waiting for everyone to descend. The men in here are now whispers that disperse, each one to his own thing, one to the head, another possibly to the galley for coffee, others to bed. I climb up again, look out on deck. Morán and Polski are still at the dock, sitting on the ground in the circle of light, their backs resting against a wall. Morán has placed the carton of cigarettes between them and at this moment is tugging on the paper wrapper; he struggles a little till he tears it and pulls out a pack, which he hands to Polski, then he takes one for himself and starts to open it while Polski opens his own; the scene plays out symmetrically. Morán takes out a lighter at the same time Polski takes out a lighter. Morán lights his cigarette at the same time Polski tries to light his, but as it turns out, he fails in his effort and for a moment the symmetry is broken. It's humid, how strange, huh? and he smiles at Morán as he stashes his useless lighter in his pants pocket. Morán offers him his own lighter, which Polski accepts in his gigantic hands, he lights his cigarette on the first try and returns it to Morán; both of them puff now, and white plumes, as thick as the fog that was with us throughout our crossing, rise in incredibly parallel corkscrews. They smoke, talk, laugh, talk some more, and it all reaches me like a lost echo. I stand there looking up, a light breeze stirs, sweeping a cloud away and allowing me to see a star, and who knows why it occurs to me that it's the last one, though I don't know of what, maybe just the last and only star this night, because now a line of clarity tints the horizon over the sea behind me and dawn begins to break. I turn my attention back to Polski and Morán. There are several empty packs of cigarettes rolled up in a ball on the floor in the space that separates one from the other; a lot of time must have gone by without my realizing it. Now they get up clumsily, they must be numb from this cold May night, the extended calm, the hard ground. They bend down, pick up the empty packs, go over to a trash can a few steps away from the light post and throw them in there, light another couple of cigarettes with Morán's lighter and start walking away from the sub. They walk away slowly, along the path that leads to the Stella Maris Chapel. They're going to pray, no doubt, they're going to talk some more and smoke some more. And then they'll come back and they'll say goodbye at the dock, and Polski will go up to the deck of the sub and down the ladder, and Morán will stay on the dock for a while looking at the dark outline of the *San Luis*, trying to understand what this business of being in a war must be like.

The others are putting their things away in their bags, silently, there's no noise, jokes, snatches of old songs, nothing but the sound of the machinist folding or squeezing and stashing each one of his things in his bag. The forward hatch is open, it's nighttime again, lately it seems like it's always nighttime, an endless night. Suddenly, someone who's just come aboard says that a bus is waiting for us, parked in the shadow of the shadows, a bus that will take us to Mar del Plata. It's not like we're criminals who have to hide, says Polski under his breath. Nobody opens their mouths, not one word crosses those closed lips, but the air grows thick with unspoken assent as they continue stashing their things, some of them already pulling on the cords that close the mouths of their bags, others zipping up their jackets to face the even colder cold to come. Silently they wait, standing in the corridor, their bodies barely resting against the edges of the rows of bunks, their heads looking at the tips of the boots that most of them didn't wear during the crossing but have put on now. Little by little they emerge, bags slung over shoulders, boots advancing heavily along the corridor, then stepping heavily on the metal rungs of the forward ladder, one step and another step and another step, and another man and another step and another step and another man, the pounding repeating again and again as the sub empties out. I smooth my overalls, the last in line, I walk slowly forward. Next to the torpedoes, Grunwald makes way for Heredia, who starts to ascend; behind Grunwald, Olivero appears, carrying my boots in one hand by the top opening, his bag slung over the opposite shoulder. I stand there watching him, not understanding, as if seeing him with my boots was itself a question, the question I've needed to ask since God knows when but didn't ask. What's with those boots? Grunwald intercepts him, as the last men climb up and leave. They're Ortega's boots, they've been here since that day, they made the whole crossing with us, Olivero replies. And why are you taking them? Grunwald asks, patting the fake wire glasses stashed in his jacket pocket. I'm bringing them to his wife, or his mother, I think they'll want to have them, Olivero replies, looking at the dark dent at the tip of my boot. It's strange, isn't it? Grunwald adds, It's as if he ... as if he ... well, you know I believe in that stuff ... but don't pay any attention to me. Are you going up? You first, says Olivero, and while Grunwald climbs and now—from down here—you can only see his boots, Olivero looks me in the eye and completes the sentence that had remained unfinished: It's as if he'd been with us all the time. And then he begins to climb the ladder, too, I see him go up rung by rung till he flows into the night up there. Someone closes the ladder from the outside and I get the feeling I should be confused, but oddly enough I'm not; I remain there staring upward for a while without summoning the energy to do anything, and now, suddenly, I walk toward the galley, not knowing exactly why till I get there and stand before the open door. Even though it seems ridiculous, I look for the surviving jar of capers, I look on the counter, in the cupboards, in the drawers, but it's not there. Then I go to my bed; the sheets are tangled, just as I left them, the book open to the last page. I climb into my bunk; any minute now the lights will go off, so meanwhile I take advantage of the time to read a little: the animal has reached a point where he doesn't want to know anything for sure, he's satisfied with choosing a nice chunk of skinned red meat and he curls up on a pile of dirt, at least there will be some silence and he'll be able to dream all he wants. But I can't go on, my lids are heavy, and I understand that I'll end up falling asleep pretty soon, asleep with the question, tired as I am from walking around and not finding anything.

ABOUT PATRICIA RATTO

PATRICIA RATTO is an Argentine writer and teacher. She is the author of the novels *Pequeños hombres blancos* (*Little White Men*, 2006), *Nudos* (*Knots*, 2008), and *Trasfondo* (*Background*, 2012) and the story collection *Faunas* (*Wildlife*, 2017), all published by Adriana Hidalgo Editora. Many of her short stories have been published in literary magazines and anthologies, while her novels have previously been translated into Italian, and her novella, *Trasfondo*, is scheduled to be turned into a feature film by award-winning Argentine director Pablo Giorgelli. *Proceed With Caution* is her English language debut.

ABOUT ANDREA G. LABINGER

ANDREA G. LABINGER has published numerous translations of Latin American fiction. *Gesell Dome*, her translation of Guillermo Saccomanno's noir novel *Cámara Gesell* (Open Letter, 2016), won a PEN/Heim Translation Award and was long-listed for the Community of Literary Magazines and Presses' Firecracker Award. Her most recent translation, Saccomanno's *77* (Open Letter 2019) was selected as a finalist for the 2020 Best Translated Book Awards.